OUR FATHER'S
SPIRIT

OUR FATHER'S SPIRIT

LEAH D. TURNER

TATE PUBLISHING
AND **ENTERPRISES, LLC**

Published by Tate Publishing & Enterprises, LLC
127 E. Trade Center Terrace | Mustang, Oklahoma 73064 USA
1.888.361.9473 | www.tatepublishing.com

Tate Publishing is committed to excellence in the publishing industry. The company reflects the philosophy established by the founders, based on Psalm 68:11,
"The Lord gave the word and great was the company of those who published it."

Book design copyright © 2016 by Tate Publishing, LLC. All rights reserved.
Cover design by Albert Ceasar Compay
Interior design by Gram Telen

Published in the United States of America

ISBN: 978-1-68207-970-6
1. Fiction / African American / Christian
2. Fiction / African American / Urban
15.10.19

This book is dedicated to the true and living God…the One who gave it to me. I thank Him for giving me to Roma Nell Edwards Turner. My mother. She never gave up on me no matter how bad the situation was. She was my Scribe for a while during this process. Thanks mom, you're awesome! This is the result of a praying mother. Thanks to my baby Ophrah Ziniah…the "song bird" She has been quite the actress reading my lines. Thanks to Candace LaShonn, the badest Armor Bearer in the land! Couldn't have finished without you. God put you where you needed to be! And Jay-B Baby, my soldier in training. I love my family…the family the God made.

This book is also dedicated to the lost ones, the ones walking around unconscious. Our Father is big and great and He will deliver!

1

The smell of fried chicken and cigarettes permeates the air.

"Girl, you need to stop smokin' them cigarettes! It ain't good, smokin' around these babies like that! I can hardly stand it…so I know they can't!" exclaimed Grandma Rose as she stood at the stove, turning her fried chicken. "The only reason I'm standing here frying this chicken is because of those three baby boys over there! You done disappointed me, so 'till I don't hardly know what to do but turn your sorry behind over to the Lord!" Rose exclaimed, getting revved up as she did on a daily basis. "I better not do that no more! I turned you over to the Lord, and when I knew anything, here comes Elijah being born! Running around with that no-count supposed-to-be man of God that I sent you to for counseling to get you on the right track! He got you on the right track all right! Slipping and sliding from motel to motel! I could hardly show my face around here, I was so ashamed! Everybody was talking about it!" Rose said forcefully.

"Mama, hush! You always talkin' about what the Lord gonna do! What has He done?" Rose May exclaimed. "We ain't got nothing! We living in the ghetto, we ain't got no car, and we broke as hell! What He done, Ma? That's why I gotta get out here and do what I gotta do!" Rose May yelled. "You think He just gonna rain money from the sky?" Rose May asked with a big attitude.

Rose just continued on frying her chicken and rolling her eyes at her once beautiful and content daughter.

Rose May was named after her mother Rose. Both women were beautiful; there was just fifteen-year difference in their age.

Grandma Rose was about five feet six inches tall, with a caramel complexion and long sandy hair that fell halfway her back. Even though she was African-American, she had Native American traits that were very dominant. She also had a set of full, naturally red lips that curved into a slight pout when she smiled. Her lips were so red when she was born that her mother looked upon her and whispered the name Rose just before she died.

At fifteen, Rose became pregnant with Rose May and was sent down South by her father to live with relatives in the Abernathy projects. After the baby was born, she named her Rose May because she looked so much like her, and she was born on May 2.

Even though Rose was an extremely young mother, she gladly accepted the responsibilities that came with motherhood and raised Rose May with very little help from others. She became disillusioned with men after Rose May's father because she really thought she was in love with him. After she realized that every sweet nothing that he whispered to her was truly nothing, she dove wholeheartedly into her daughter. Rose dated a few men off and on with encouragement from her aunts, but she was never in love again—except with her daughter, Rose May. She loved the very ground on which she walked. She worked her fingers to the bone for Rose May, sometimes working two or three jobs, fourteen and fifteen hour days to make ends meet and to get Rose May what she wanted.

Aunt Minnie, Rose's aunt, kept Rose May while Rose worked all those horrendous hours. Aunt Minnie ran the local liquor house that serviced the neighborhood and all surrounding hoods. Aunt Minnie had all sorts of characters in and out of her establishment. Aunt Minnie loved a dollar, and selling liquor certainly came before Rose May. Minnie often told Rose, "You need ta stop workin' for dem ol' white folks, an' come work wit' me! You ain't makin' no real money. Good a lookin' woman as you is, I know you can fin' yoself a man an' a daddy for Rose May! Workin' yo fangers to the bone…fuh what? You 'bout to work yoself to death!" Minnie bellowed loudly. "And if that ain't enough, you done ran over there an' hooked up wit' them ol Bibletotin' wannabe-like Christians at that church around the corner! Them ol' deacons be around here huntin' a drank a liquor and a woman all in the same day!"

Everyone who knew Rose and Aunt Minnie thought they were sisters; they had been together so long. But all they had to do was look at the difference in the two. Aunt Minnie was short dark-skinned nappy-headed and never had a lack for words. She had a common-law husband whose name was Malichi, but everybody called him Uncle Mookie. He was quiet and reserved until Friday night when he got home and got his first drink for the weekend. Uncle Mookie came to life! The first thing he did was give Aunt Minnie his paycheck when he came through the door. The patrons at the house would joke and say that was his ticket to stay another week.

Once the fish started frying, the cards started slapping on the table, and the whiskey started flowing, Uncle Mookie would start. "Minnie don't do nothing but take all my damn money," he would say in a drunken slur. "She don't care nothing 'bout me, she just want all my money."

Minnie would hustle and bustle around, serving liquor to the guests, fixing fish and chicken sandwiches, popping open cans of beer, and even being flirtatious with a few of the patrons especially the big spenders, until she could take all she could take of Mookie's mouth. She would stop what she was doing, put her hands on her hips, and give Uncle Mookie a piece of her mind. But not before warning him.

"Mookie, now you better go on an' leave me alone now! I don't feel like this shit! I'm tired of your shit! You love to show out when folks come! Now, somebody goin' to jail or hell one tonight!" Minnie would say.

Everybody would keep right on eating their greasy fish or chicken sandwiches, throwing their shots back, chugging their beers, and puffing on their smokes because this was business as usual at Aunt Minnie's liquor house on Friday night.

take over my business and take care of me when I can't do around. Rose May gone be a pretty young thang when she come to herself. She a lil' chunky right now, but you wait. I can see it," Aunt Minnie would hiss to Uncle Mookie.

"Now, Minnie, you leave that gal alone! I see 'zackly what you doin', and it just ain't right!" Mookie pleaded.

"She gon' bring me some money in here! They is two things I knows about, that's my mens and my money!" Minnie hollered, slapping her big black thigh.

Rose May, like her mother, was gorgeous. She had cinnamon-colored skin, and her eyes were the color of grey marbles, shaped like almonds. Her cheeks were adorned with dimples as deep as ditches, and her mouth formed into a perfect oval shape. Her beautiful brown hair with auburn streaks fell slightly below her shoulders.

During the day, Aunt Minnie also sold candy to the neighborhood kids. So Rose May began to get chubby as a result of her endless supply of confections, by helping herself to the stockpile of goodies. She could eat all day every day if she chose to. Not to mention the fish and chicken sandwiches fried in pure lard. They weren't just cooked on the weekends; you could always depend on a good hot meal at Aunt Minnie's house.

For breakfast, Rose May could look forward to hot buttery pancakes, fresh homemade biscuits from the oven, that could be used to sop up the thick Grandma's Molasses with chunks of butter mashed in them with a fork. Most times, Aunt Minnie would fry up some pork chops, sausage, or bacon to go with the aforementioned delicacies.

Rose May loved to eat! The food took the place of her mother's absence and comforted her when she felt so alone.

"Lawd, have mercy! You shole is getting big, Rose May! You too fat!" Aunt Minnie yelled, as if she had seen Rose May for the first time. "You got a pretty face, you just too fat!" she ranted. "You need to get out an' be with them other children! Staying in the house wit' yo nose in a book all the time! You know that ain't no way to do! What's wrong wit' you?" Aunt Minnie asked, not giving the girl time to answer. She continued, "Here, you is just twelve years old and wide as all outside!" Minnie continued, "Yo mamma mentioned something about that to me, but I didn't pay her no attention. This my damn kitchen, and I can run it any way I sees fit!" she exclaimed feverishly. "Hell, if it wasn't for me, she couldn't work like she do! She better stay out my damn business! I don't charge her one damn dime for keepin' you! Hell, she used to offer, but now she done stopped that! So she best stay out my damn face 'cause as long as you under this roof, you is my business! And you gone mess that up by being too damn fat! I got big plans for you, gal!" Minnie shouted as she chugged her ice-cold beer and sauntered off.

Rose May was devastated. All she could hear was Aunt Minnie's ratchet voice in her head over and over again, telling her how useless, ugly, and fat she was. It just wouldn't go away! Until then, Rose May hadn't felt that anything was wrong with her; but after her encounter with Aunt Minnie, she not only felt useless, ugly, and fat, she also felt abandoned by her mother. That night, when Rose May undressed and stood in front of her old broken down dresser mirror, she saw something too horrendous to describe! She climbed in her cold lonely bed and sobbed until her pillow was wet.

3

Even though Rose May was the finest-dressed girl in the neighborhood (her mother saw to that), she began to notice that all the other girls had boyfriends runnin' in behind em' as Aunt Minnie would say, but her.

The school year ended, and Rose May decided she would go on a diet for the entire summer.

She began turning down Aunt Minnie's homemade delicacies and began riding the new bicycle her mother had rewarded her with for getting good grades that school year. She also started hanging out with a few new friends and saw that the boys were giving her some much-needed attention because she was losing a little weight.

Very seldom did Rose May spend quality time with her mother, so she savored every moment that this occurred. On this particular day, they spent the entire day together doing girl stuff. As Rose was brushing her daughter's long beautiful hair, she decided it would be a good time for them to have the woman talk because she had recently started her period.

"Rose May," Rose said in a very loving voice, "I know I haven't been around a lot for you, but I had to work so you could have all the nice things I didn't have when I was a child." Rose continued, "That's why we go to church every Sunday that I'm off because I know the good Lord is keeping you. He answered my prayers already. I know I didn't want you to grow up all big and fat, and you know you are looking good now. I'm so proud of you baby, I want you to go to college and be somebody. That's why I work so hard." Rose said, almost in tears, "I know Minnie's ain't the best place for you, but she love you. She been with us from the very day you was born. When I got off that bus thirteen years ago, I felt like a ole dirty dishrag that had been throwed out with the ol' dirty dishwater. Don't nobody but God know how I felt that day. Coming down South, leaving my daddy, and on top of that, leaving yours!" Rose lamented and exclaimed, "Lord, I guess that's why Jesus is my daddy now! He ain't failed me yet! I didn't even see your daddy when I went back for the funeral."

Rose May interrupted. "How old was I then, Ma?"

"You was a little bitty thing when my daddy died, about two. And your daddy didn't even come to the house to see you." Rose said sorrowfully. "Honey, let me tell you one thing," Rose continued, visibly perturbed. "Please don't put your trust and faith in no sorry-ass man on this earth! He will disappoint you every time! They will lie to you, cheat on you, even steal from you! So please, please promise me you won't mess up with no man!" Rose snapped and walked off visibly upset.

That was the end of their mother-daughter talk. Case closed, no questions asked, none answered. After all, it was Aunt Minnie who helped Rose May when she got her monthly. Her idea about men was totally different than Rose's.

"Money, honey! That's all I want!" Aunt Minnie always repeated. "It take money to make the world go round, and it take money to make Minnie go up and down!" she said, rolling her big wide flabby hips. "If you go to bed with a man, make for sho you gets up with more than a wet behind… some money, or you'll be workin' like a po dog all yo life like yo Ma. I'm gonna teach you about life and what make the world go round," Minnie would state very matter-of-factly. "Now run tell that!" Minnie cackled before finishing her half can of Miller beer with one gigantic gulp, followed by a titanic belch.

When school started after the summer break, Rose May was the talk of the neighborhood and school. She had managed to lose about twenty-five pounds by turning down Aunt Minnie's good homemade cooking, bike riding with some friends she had met. And while watching a show on television, she saw a girl about her age eating as much as she wanted, then sticking her fingers down her throat and throwing up, and she looked great! Rose May was happy. They called it binging and purging. She thought it was the coolest thing she had ever seen. An answer to all her problems. She could have her cake and eat it too! As much as she wanted!

4

With confidence, Rose May went about her daily chores at Aunt Minnie's house. When I say chores, I don't mean sweeping, mopping, and dusting. Rose May learned early on that it was impossible to keep a liquor house clean, so she did just enough to satisfy Aunt Minnie, who was too busy mingling or, as she put it, getting dat dollah to pay attention to Rose May's domestic duties. The other chores consisted of keeping the glasses clean (if you know what I mean), keeping the ashtrays emptied (if you know what I mean), eating as much as possible, sticking her finger down her throat, and purging.

The "regulars" in the house began to take a second look at Rose May. No longer was she the cute little chubby girl with pigtails standing before them. That summer launched a new season for Rose May. She had filled out quite nicely. She was wearing her jeans tighter and her skirts shorter. Aunt Minnie's business was hot! And so was Rose May!

"Giiiiiirl, you know you fine!" Aunt Minnie proclaimed, showing off her four shiny gold teeth that introduced her wide smile. "You got a moneymaker on you!" Minnie exclaimed, grabbing Rose May's hand, holding it high over her head and twirling her around like a prima ballerina. "I knowed you had something up under all that fat! I knowed it!" she exclaimed very excitedly. "I done took care of you all this time. I ain't charge yo ma one damn dime…not one red cent! Now it's the big payback time…ha! You is good! You is so, so good!" Minnie yelped, swaying drunk in the doorway.

"Look, Mookie! Look at my baby, ain't she fiiiine?" Minnie stammered as Uncle Mookie entered the room.

Mookie looked up at Minnie clearly agitated about her drunken state. "Minnie, I done tol' you to leave that gal alone now! I knows what you doin', an it just ain't right! An I'm gone tell Rose befo' it get outa hand!" Mookie threatened.

Aunt Minnie shot Mookie a glance of daggers before saying, "You shut the heeeell up, Mookie! This be my kinfolk! Sides, I don't see you goin' nowhere! You shole is happy round here! I don't see you turnin' nothing down, but yo dingy-ass collar!" Minnie yelled, snapping her neck, rolling her eyes, and lighting up a cigarette.

"Trouble, trouble, trouble," Mookie mumbled under his gin-soaked breath. "And I ain't gonna have nothin' to do wit' nothin'," Mookie said, exiting through the front door, slamming it so hard the faded print on the wall of Martin Luther King shook.

Aunt Minnie trailed after him, yelling across the yard, "Don't be slammin' no damn doughs round here! I don't know why I put up wit' the same ol' shit day after day wit' that man. I'm tired…just tired!" Minnie snarled as she sat down in her captain's chair.

She called the chair her "captain's chair" because that's where she primarily served all her patrons, made her change, smoked her Winston 100 cigarettes, drank her beloved Schlitz Malt Liquor, kept her eyes on the tunk and pitty-pat tables to make sure she got her cut game, ate an occasional fish or chicken sandwich, and recurrently got dead drunk.

Rose May didn't pay Minnie's drunk mouth any attention. She was busy focusing on all the chores she had lined up. She just stood there and grinned dumbly. Not because she was dumb, but because she was tipsy. Minnie was too busy seeing dollar signs to discern Rose May's condition.

"You ain't got to tell yo ma everything we talk about neither. You ain't no fool," Minnie chided. "I'm gonna put you on some pills, fool around, and come up big, and Rose will be lookin' sideways at me. I been knowing Rose too long to fall out behind some fast-tailed gal!" Minnie scolded.

Rose May was wishing Aunt Minnie would hurry and finish her good-talkin'-to, as she called it, so she could go fix her a stiff drink. She had now moved up from corners to actual shots!

Rose May would ignore him when she was at school with her friends.

"Aw, Tony, don't act like that. You know it ain't even like that. I be seeing you," Rose May said coaxingly.

"Well, why don't you ever let me walk you to class or carry your books or nothing?" Tony whined.

Rose May was really getting tired of going in these circles with Tony, but she had to pick him for information.

"Tooonyyy," Rose May said unsympathetically, ignoring his pleas."I called to ask you about somebody," Rose May blurted out between his pleas.

"Who?" he asked in a sulky tone.

"That boy you and—"

Tony cut her off before she could finish the sentence. "I already know who you gone ask me about," Tony said gloomily.

"You didn't even let me finish," Rose May unremittingly replied.

"I don't need to let you finish. Every girl in the hood been asking about New York!" Tony replied, clearly agitated.

"New York?" Rose May said, sounding as if she was seeing stars.

Obviously, Tony heard it in her voice too because he got mad. The next thing Rose May heard was a dial tone in her ear.

"That ol' stupid boy!" Rose May said aloud, sucking her teeth. "He's just jealous I don't wanna go with him," she said as she plopped down on her bed to watch *Good Times* and smoke a shorted out Vantage cigarette.

Just as she was about to light the crushed-up end of the cigarette, Aunt Minnie barreled into her room.

"Rose May, some boy out here to see you," she announced with a sly grin, showing her sparkly gold fronts.

"Who?" Rose May asked, looking puzzled. She wasn't dating anybody even though Aunt Minnie wanted her to. She knew her mother didn't approve, and she didn't want to risk being caught by her.

Rose May was still a good girl at this point.

"Some fine lil' fella smellin' all good. He say he name Tony," Aunt Minnie stated in a drunken slur. "You been takin' them pills I got you, ain't you?" Minnie asked.

Rose May just pushed her way past Minnie, rolled her eyes to the top of her head, and sucked her teeth.

"Awww, heeeelll naw!" Minnie garbled, grabbing Rose May by the arm. "You ain't gone sass me gal! I don't care how grown or fine you think you is…this my damn house, and I'll knock yo head off! You hear me?" Minnie huffed like a big bull.

"Yes, mam," Rose May said, looking up at Aunt Minnie like a scared kitten.

One thing Rose May learned early on was that you do not, under any circumstances, sass Aunt Minnie, unless you are willing to go to war and fight to the death.

"That's more like it," Minnie smiled and said. "Now go on an' see yo fine lil' boyfriend." Minnie said, snapping back to her happy drunk mode.

"He ain't my boyfriend, Aunt Minnie," Rose May whined.

"Child, hush." Minnie replied, reaching in her apron pocket, pulling out an ice-cold Schlitz, popping the top and snapping her fat fingers to the music.

Rose May pushed her way through the cigarette smoke, tinkling glasses, curse words being hurled back and forth, and the cluster of people on the so-called linoleum dance floor that was scuffed up to no end. Once she reached the end of the maze of Friday night partyers, she saw Tony standing there, looking through the hazy crowd, anticipating her appearance.

"What you want boy?" Rose May asked, rolling her eyes.

"Come outside and talk to me, Rosey," Tony pleaded, batting his long eyelashes.

Rose May had to admit he was cute, and the Polo cologne he was wearing did smell good. He still ain't as cute as that chocolate-skinned boy, Rose May thought to herself.

Tony followed Rose May outside, and they sat on the porch swing.

"And stop calling me Rosey!" Rose May said as they proceeded to the porch swing.

"I need to talk to you alone Rosey...I mean Rose May," Tony said.

"We are alone," Rose May giggled as she playfully punched Tony's arm.

"No we ain't," Tony solemnly stated.

Well, they really were alone, except for the occasional inebriated partygoer who staggered on to the porch, the two secret lovers who sneaked out to steal a clandestine moment, or somebody who came out to smoke a joint or two.

"We alone as we gon' be, Tony, 'cause if my momma come up, you gon' wish we was invisible," Rose May announced, looking around cautiously.

"Rose May, you know I like you. How you gon' call me askin' 'bout that ol' pretty boy New York? You know I been likin' you since we was in first grade. I used to always give you my juice and cookies," Tony whined.

"Shut up, that was kid stuff. You and me gon' always be tight," Rose May said, giving Tony a "buddy hug rather than a boyfriend-hug. He seemed to be more than pleased because he gave her all the information she wanted, and then some. Tony had been wrapped around Rose May's finger for a long time.

"His name is Bobby…Bobby Miller. But they call him New York 'cause he's from up the road…New York City," Tony continued as Rose May listened attentively. "He got in some kind of trouble up there, so his momma sent him down here to live with his grandma," Tony said, lighting up a KOOL cigarette.

"When you start smoking, Tony?" Rose May asked, leaning back looking at him.

"Everybody smoke now, girl," Tony replied, taking a long draw of his cigarette.

"I know. Give me one," Rose May said, holding up a BIC lighter she had swiped from Aunt Minnie's stash. They both laughed as Tony handed her a cigarette. She lit up, and they inhaled together.

"You don't need to mess with that boy, Rose May," Tony warned. "He's too slick for you. That dude gets high and everthing," Tony said, blowing smoke out of his nose.

"You do too," Rose May replied. "I know you and June Bug be smokin' reefer all the time," she said, pointing her cigarette-laden finger at him.

"I know, I know. But he be doing serious stuff…powder!" Tony said, scrunching his nose up. "What you want with him? He ain't better than me!" Tony said, throwing his hands in the air.

"I don't know, Tony," Rose May said, throwing her cigarette down, crushing it under her shiny new penny loafer. "It's just something about a boy from up the road, Tony!" Rose May said emphatically. "Aunt Minnie was talking about that the other day."

"You and Aunt Minnie both gon' get in a world of trouble messing with them up the road niggas. You and everybody else know Aunt Minnie ain't got no sense. You better leave Aunt Minnie and her crazy ass alone! She's a fool!" Tony stated emphatically. "Ever since you lost that weight, you ain't been the same. Sometimes I wish you was still fat, at least you would listen to somebody!" Tony said, all up in her face.

Rose May just sat there pouting, looking down at her new penny loafers with shiny new pennies in them. She knew that look would break him down, so she just admired her shoes while she waited.

Tony sucked his teeth after a few moments of silence and said, "I see you ain't gon' listen, so I'll holler at him and see what's up."

Rose May looked up at him, batting her pretty gray eyes and planted a big wet kiss on his lips.

"Don't get too happy, I might change my mind," Tony said as he hopped down off the porch.

Rose May didn't say a word as she watched Tony leave. She knew that he had promised to do something for her that he really didn't want to do. This would only be one of the many things Tony would do for her that he didn't want to do. That's how much he loved her.

5

The party was on tonight! Aunt Minnie was in rare form—full party mode. Sometimes she would parade around the house in a pretty nightgown and housecoat set to entertain her guests because if her "money was lookin' funny," as she would say, she would have to lay up with a few of her regulars and "roll they pockets." Of course, these "regulars" would have to be totally smashed to "lay up" with Aunt Minnie. But after a few shots of Aunt Minnie's homebrew, to them, she looked like a darker version of Lena Horne. That homebrew was some powerful stuff!

Minnie would prance around like she was Miss Liquor House America, all dolled up in her best nightclothes with a pair of what she called her "Sunday go to meetin'" shoes on. Minnie would say she was not only dressed for success, but dressed to get blessed. After making such a proclamation, Minnie would fire up a Winston 100, put it between her brightly painted lips, take a long draw, exhale, down a shot or two of gin, sit back in her "captain's chair," try to cross her big ham hock of a leg, and grin widely, showing off her lipstick-stained gold teeth.

Minnie lied on, "Hell, if you get enough liquor in a nigga, he'll think he in the bed wit' Lena Horn or Eartha Kitt! Don't matter none to me, long as I gets me me!"

Aunt Minnie was getting wound up as she sipped her gin and juice, chasing it with her beloved Schlitz Malt Liquor. She continued on, walking the floor by now.

"Minnie start wit' M, an so do money! My momma knowed what she was doin' when she named me Minnie! Minnie, money, Minnie money," she repeated over and over again in a drunken slur. "M and M...that's me! Just like Marilyn Monroe! Her name start wit' M too! She got the same letters startin' both her names!" Minnie slurred, turning up an empty can of Schlitz. "Bring me another beer!" Minnie yelled to Rose May, who was at the stove, frying fish.

"Aunt Minnie, I can't leave the stove right now!" Rose May yelled back, barely audible because of the music and the laughter generated from Minnie's performance.

Minnie almost fell over with razor in hand while trying to dance seductively to Marvin Sease's "Candy Licker" that was blaring on the old rickety hi-fi.

"Minnie!" Uncle Mookie hollered as she stumbled and fell in his lap on her last "Dirty Dancing With the Stars" twirl. "You need to set yo fat ass down, Minnie! Put that damn razor up befo' you hurt somebody!" Mookie hollered very sternly.

Everyone knew that if Mookie hadn't been two sheets to the wind, there is no way he would have had the balls to speak to Aunt Minnie that way...she usually kept his balls in her apron pocket, especially when Minnie had her rusty razor in hand.

"How in the hell you gone see after thangs in the shape you in?" Mookie questioned. "You done got bad, Minnie, baaad!" Mookie said, shaking his head, continuing to fuss. "Somebody got to have some damn sense around here! Shiiiit! I can't even drink in peace no mo'. You gon' let folks come up in here and run off wit' everything we got! I puts in too! We ain't gon' have shit if it be left up to yo, wild ass!" Mookie was dead serious, and he didn't shut up. Uncle Mookie had to make just one more of his observations known. Minnie just sat in a drunken stupor. "I been seeing all them ol' young dope boys hanging 'round here. They say they be up in them gangs and sellin' dope and stuff!" Mookie stated very ardently. "Now what the hell they doing up in here? I know you don't think you can keep up wit' that crowd! They'll kill you just as soon as look at you!" Mookie said, taking another swig of his liquid courage, continuing to rant sluggishly in his drunken state. He didn't know how prophetic his statement was.

Rose May had finished her fish-cooking shift for the night. There were still a few stragglers in the front, but

Rose May was tired. She was ready to get her drink on. She headed back to her room, but not before grabbing a couple of pints of knottyhead gin from Aunt Minnie's stash that she called her cut bottles. She knew Aunt Minnie was nice and passed out by now, and Uncle Mookie was holding down the front as best he could. There were only two regulars up front with him, Flip and Scobo, and they were Mookie's cousins.

Rose May entered her liquor house/penthouse suite and surveyed the premises. She had to admit it was pretty fly, considering its location. Rose had tried to make it as comfortable as possible for Rose May since she was always there. Her room at Aunt Minnie's was nicer than her room at her mother's house. Rose May had a queen-size bed with a matching curtain and comforter set, nice fluffy pillows, a big vanity table, a 25" color TV with an Atari, a Sony component set with a turntable and double cassette deck, a big comfy chair, a nightstand with a swag lamp over it, and a big purple shag rug on the floor.

Rose May plopped down in her big comfy chair, cracked open her bottle of gin, took a big gulp, and smacked her lips. Just as Rose May popped in her S.O.S. Band cassette, packed her fresh pack of KOOL 100s on the back of her hand, she heard a tap on her window. She walked over, peeped out, and much to her surprise, it was the pretty chocolate-skinned boy. Rose May lifted up the window with her gin bottle securely tucked under her arm.

"What's up, shorty? I heard you wanted to holler at me," the dark silhouette said.

Rose May just stood there for a moment, listening to the trancelike sounding words coming from the prettiest set of lips she had ever seen on a boy. She just loved the way people from up the road sounded.

"So what's up, shorty?" the beguiling voice chimed in again.

Rose May was thunderstruck! She just cocked her head to the side and watched his mouth moving.

"You can talk, can't you? Must be that gin you got tucked under your arm working on your pretty little head. Can I have some?" the well-dressed, good-smelling handsome young man said, climbing on in the window without an invitation.

Rose May stepped back and handed him the bottle as if in a trance. "Uuuh, uuh, yeah…you can have some," she stammered slowly, sweeping over his tight muscular frame with her mouth wide open. *Wow!* Rose May thought, licking her lips lustfully, *He sure is one fine dude.*

"I'm Bobby…Bobby Miller. But everybody call me New York," he said, unscrewing the cap on the gin bottle and taking a big swig. "I can tell we're going to get along real, real good, shorty," Bobby surmised.

Rose May still hadn't said anything. She was too busy ogling her newfound drinking buddy.

New York was about five foot ten; he had thick black curly hair that was shaped in the most perfectly boxed high-topped fade Rose May had ever seen. In the back of his head, he had a perfect symmetrically shaped NY. New York had a set of sleepy bedroom eyes that looked like two black limpid pools. His nose was strong, stern, and it flared slightly around the edges. Underneath his nose was a wispy, perfectly shaped mustache that met the edges of his luscious moist lips. Between those luscious moist lips was a set of stunning white teeth with a gold tooth on the side that peeped out when he smiled. Beneath his bottom lip was a chin that housed a deep dimple.

What a dreamboat! Rose May thought as she continued to survey the young man.

Underneath his button-down polo shirt was a set of broad shoulders and a well-chiseled chest that was the resting place for a thick gold-roped chain. The shirt was tucked in to a perfect size 32 pair of heavily starched Levi's jeans, with a crease that would cut butter. The jean's cuffs relaxed on a pair of penny loafers with dimes in them.

"Whew!" Rose May said aloud after drinking in the scrumptious boy candy.

Rose May thought she'd said that in her head because New York asked, "What's wrong, little mommie? You must have started sipping way before me, huh? You ain't said five words since I came in. You ain't scared, are you?" he asked, pulling out a small brown envelope. "You one fine little momma. I saw you checking me out the other day when I rode by. I asked my man Tony about you. He act like he got heated or something…Y'all ain't talking or nothing, are you?" he asked, fumbling through his Members Only jacket pocket.

"No!" Rose May said, making sure New York could see her adamant facial expression. "I don't know what's wrong wit' him. We been tight since the first grade…I guess he just lookin' out," she said, grabbing her not-so-freshly-opened bottle of gin.

"Can I cop a squat?" New York asked, grabbing the cover of Rose May's Michael Jackson's *Off the Wall* album cover to dump the contents of his little brown envelope on.

"What you doin', cuz?" Rose May asked, screwing up her face. "Don't be disrespecting my stuff! You don't even know if I smoke reefer, let alone allow it on my premises!" she said, rolling her neck, lighting up her KOOL 100, and robustly inhaling.

"Come on now, shorty," he said, moving seductively closer to Rose May.

When she took a whiff of the pungent aromatic cologne, all she could do was sink down in her big cushy chair and give a hypnotic nod of yes.

"I know peeps be around here smoking herb. Shiiiiit, this a liquor spot," New York said, commencing to lick his two "top" papers, stick the wet ends together, fold them, reach over and grab the weed from Michael Jackson's face, and proceed to roll.

Rose May watched as New York sat on her bed, finished rolling the fat joint, and gently moistened it by placing it between his two beautiful, luscious lips. This was the first time Rose May had ever had any dealings with pot. The most she had ever done was drink a little gin or beer and smoke her cigarettes. As New York fired up the twisted blend of weeds, stems, and dried leaves, Rose May inhaled the overpowering smoke that rushed from his mouth as he exhaled.

"This some good herb, shortie. Go ahead, take a pull," New York said, stretching his jeweled hand forth like a snake charmer.

Rose May reached forth and plucked the joint from his hand, stared at it as if she were under a spell, put it to her rosy lips, and inhaled slowly. While holding the smoke in, she threw her head back, closed her eyes, and exhaled. When she opened her eyes, New York was in her face, nose-to-nose. Rose May felt his hot, steamy reefer-gin-soaked breath on her face.

"How you like that?" he said, sliding his hand over her ample backside, pulling her closer. "Go 'head, baby, take another pull," New York coaxed. "I got plenty more where that came from," he bragged.

Rose May was high, and she felt nice, real nice. She felt like a rag doll in New York's strong arms. After they sat down, took a few more tokes, drank some beer, and finished off two pints of gin, New York began to move in for the kill. He grabbed Rose May by her hand and led her to the edge of her bed.

"Hold on, Mr. up-the-road! I might be high, but I ain't that damn high!" Rose May said, snapping into Aunt Minnie mode, pushing New York away.

The one thing Aunt Minnie did teach her was not to give it up too fast.

"You ain't gon' be going out of here telling everybody you got broke off on the first night! You might as well take yo ass on!" Rose May snapped, suddenly being released from his bewitching clutch.

"All right...all right...I feel you, shortie!" New York said, throwing his hands up and backing up. "I'm gonna leave now, but I'll be back because you gonna be my girl, my shorty!" And with that being sternly said, he exited the same way he came.

Rose May looked at the window through which her future boyfriend had exited and said aloud, " Um, um, um, ooooo, he fine! I shole am gonna be your girl!" and held up her gin bottle, as if making a toast in the air.

Rose May was happy, but there was a rumble in her stomach that didn't feel right. She thought it may be the gin, beer, and reefer mixture brewing in her stomach. She would soon find out how wrong she was.

6

The sun was shining brightly; the birds were chirping, and in the distance, as Rose May cracked her eyes open, she could hear the hum of a lawn mower. Boy, did she have a massive headache! Rose May sat up in her bed and displayed a wide grin. She was thinking about her new boyfriend, New York. Her musing was interrupted by Aunt Minnie's boisterous loud laughing. Rose May scurried down the hallway to see what all the laughter was about. Much to her surprise, she saw New York sitting at the kitchen table puffing on a joint, passing it over to Aunt Minnie, who was high as a Georgia Pine.

"New York?" Rose May asked, as if she didn't know his name. "What you doin' up in here smoking reefer with Aunt Minnie? How you know, New York?" Rose May asked, turning to New York who was just as dreamy as ever, sitting there with a white Adidas sweat suit on, a blue T-shirt underneath, and some of the cleanest, whitest Adidas tennis shoes she had ever seen, with big, wide blue shoestrings.

"Chiiild, please! I wish I had knowed about this reefer sooner, maybe I would've sold more liquor than I drunk!" Aunt Minnie said, fervently sucking on the joint New York had passed to her.

Rose May just stood there in disbelief as she watched Aunt Minnie inhale the perfectly rolled joint and blow out a thick cloud of smoke. Rose May looked over at New York as he rolled another joint. He also had a tightly rolled-up dollar bill sitting beside the envelope of reefer and wide-mouthed Mickey beer on the table.

"You still ain't answered me, New York!" Rose May said, rolling her eyes.

New York just looked at her with a big, wide grin. He put the freshly rolled joint up to his lips, lit it, and passionately pulled in the smoke before answering, "Me and Aunt Minnie got business plans, that's all. Now come on over here and give me some sugar," he said, pulling Rose May onto his lap. She had to admit he felt just as good as he smelled.

"Here, take a taste of this," New York said after he unfolded the tightly wrapped dollar bill, licked and dipped his jeweled pinky finger in it.

"What's that?" Rose May asked as she leaned back and crinkled up her nose.

Rose May had never seen cocaine, except on *Miami Vice*.

"Here," New York urged as he pulled her closer. "Put a little of this on your tongue," he said, gripping her waist tighter.

The grip he had on Rose May's butt must have put her in a trance because before she knew it, she was sticking her tongue out. As soon as the powder fell on her tongue, Rose May instantly knew she liked it! It was a taste she had never tasted before. Her mouth felt cool and numb as she rubbed her tongue back and forth over her front teeth.

"How you like that, shorty?" New York asked as he sat there grinning, nodding his head up and down.

"I like it...I like it a lot," Rose May said, still trying to feel her teeth and gums.

"Heeeeeyyy now!" Minnie hollered as she reentered the kitchen, popping her fingers, reaching for the joint in the ashtray. "This some good shit, boy!" Minnie said, sucking down the joint as fast as she did a can of Schlitz Malt Liquor.

Rose May just sat there, stuck on New York's lap as she watched her Aunt Minnie get stoned for the first time. There was that rumble in her stomach again. Rose May just ignored it and reached for the joint that was being passed to her by her Aunt Minnie.

7

The next night about nine-thirty, Rose May heard a knock at her bedroom window. She immediately dropped the joint she was rolling and dashed to the window, pulling it up breathlessly. Not much to her surprise, it was New York. Rose May just stood there with a wide grin pasted on her face until she heard New York's voice saying, "What's up, shorty? You gonna let me in or what?"

Rose May backed up in a daze. As New York squeezed through the window, Rose May sniffed the air, taking in the aromatic fragrance of the Hugo Boss cologne he was wearing. Once in the room, Rose May scanned his tight body from head to toe. His feet were encased with, no doubt, a pair of money green Pumas that sat under a freshly starched pair of Calvin Klein jeans. On his waist was a tightly cinched-name belt that spelled out New York. His Gucci T-shirt fell nicely over his broad shoulders and gave notice to the Gucci link chain that rested heavily on his chest.

After Rose May's eyes had traveled up his body and stopped at his perfectly shaped lips, she felt a sudden jolt. New York was talking, but she hadn't heard a word he was saying; all she saw was his perfectly shaped lips moving.

"Rosie, Rosie? What's wrong, shorty? You high? You ain't hear me?" New York said, making himself comfortable in Rose May's cushy chair.

"Uuuuh no, what?" Rose May asked, regaining consciousness.

"I was saying," New York began while digging in his jean pocket, "me and Aunt Minnie fixing to make some bread up in this spot. I need you to be down with me, shorty," he said while finding the obvious treasure he had been digging for since his arrival.

Rose May noticed something different about her new boyfriend tonight. He was a little more talkative and energetic. And why was he sniffing so much? Was he catching a cold or something? And what did he keep on going to the bathroom running water for?

"What's wrong with you?" Rose May asked, watching New York take the bottom of his BIC lighter and rub it back and forth across the dollar bill that was folded longways on the table.

New York didn't answer. He just opened a book of matches, tore the back cover off, folded it to make a corner, dipped it into the dollar bill and came out with what looked like a mound of flour.

"Here. Come on," he said, reaching the "mound of flour" to Rose May.

Rose May leaned over, placed her finger over her right nostril, and inhaled the flour-like substance with a quick sniff. *Bam*! Rose May felt like a dagger hit the back of her head, and something slid down the back of her throat. Wow!

"You like that, shorty?" New York asked, displaying his immediate approval by giving Rose May another scoop to satisfy her other nostril.

"Yeeeah! I like it real good!" Rose May said, before planting a big wet kiss on New York's lips.

New York immediately pulled out a big sack of powder, and he and Rose May stayed up all night getting blowed. New York didn't realize it, but he would soon find out. He had aroused a beast with an insatiable appetite for cocaine.

8

Rose May and New York had been dating for about six months now, and during those six months, Aunt Minnie's house had become quite the spot around town. New York and his homeboys had started posting up and moving their product out of Aunt Minnie's house. Aunt Minnie didn't care as long as she was making money. There was traffic in and out all of the time. More than just the regulars began to hang out at Aunt Minnie's. New York and his boys had completely taken over!

Rose May's mother, Rose, was still busy working and hadn't noticed that Rose May, as well as Aunt Minnie, had begun to get out of hand. I know Rose didn't notice because, after all, Rose May was sixteen, going on seventeen. Rose felt like she was practically grown, and she had met New York, who seemed like a nice enough guy. Or so she thought. Rose did wonder to herself why she always had a rumble in her stomach every time she saw him on one of her few and in-between visits to Minnie's.

While Rose May was in the midst of savoring what she thought was the best high she ever had, she was interrupted.

"You all right?" Libby asked.

As Rose May lifted her head, she felt a thick drain ooze down the back of her throat. She couldn't talk. All she could do was moan.

"You want some?" Rose May asked, holding up the large bag of powder, feeling all geeked up.

"Sure," Libby replied, holding out an already folded bill.

Rose May scooped a big mound of the coke from her sack and poured it on to the bill. Libby turned swiftly and scurried down the hall like a lab rat. Rose May frowned and thought, *Something in the milk ain't clean.*

Rose May sat, and sat, and sat, waiting on Libby to emerge from the back room. Finally, Rose May got her nosy high ass up and tipped down the hall as if on a secret covert mission. Once Rose May reached the door, she smelled that smell again and heard that *click, click, click* like a lighter striking.

"Miss Libby?" Rose May's voice called out in a hard whisper. "Can I use your phone to call New York?" she asked, cupping her hand over her ear to hear. Silence. After about fifteen seconds, Libby cracked open the door, staring at Rose May with eyes of glass.

"Come on in," Libby muttered, tipping around looking down at the floor.

9

Months had passed, and Rose May had begun smoking crack on a regular basis, not to mention the immeasurable amount of beer, wine, whiskey, and reefer she was consuming. She and Libby had become fast friends because she felt safer smoking at Libby's rather than at Aunt Minnie's.

New York was at Aunt Minnie's all the time because he and Aunt Minnie had stuck a deal. New York and his boys could post up as long as they wanted, as long as Aunt Minnie got her cut. She did not care that she was now the proud owner of a liquor/dope house. She didn't care that people came in and out all times of the day and night. She didn't care that people had begun smoking crack in the back rooms. She didn't care that hookers were turning tricks in the yard. She didn't care that little baggies were strewn everywhere, and most of all she didn't care that Rose May was a zombie most of the time. Maybe she cared, but she just didn't notice. She was smashed most of the time right along with Rose May.

Because of the ferocious appetite for cocaine, Rose May was developing, she realized early on, she was not the one to be on the selling end of the game. Most times she disappeared when New York came over. After all, he was practically running the house now. He very seldom noticed that Rose May was gone. He was too busy cooking powder, snorting powder, bagging dope, smoking weed, shooting dice, and copping dates. Yes, dates. Rose May knew New York was cheating on her, but she was his main squeeze, and everybody knew it. She found out that sharing New York with the street was part of the game. She didn't care as long as she could smoke, snort, and drink all she wanted. Rose May's mother rarely checked on her because she had started working out of town. Rose May thought she had it made in the shade, drinking cool lemonade.

Minnie's spot had become really rowdy with the new crack crowd on the scene. Long gone were the days of kicking back, listening to some down home blues, having a few shots, followed by a hot greasy fish or chicken sandwich. There was hardly ever any card slapping going on anymore. No more long sultry slow drags on the faded linoleum dance floor. Flip and Scobo didn't even come around as much as a matter of fact; none of the old regulars came around much.

This new crowd was a bit much for them to handle. Uncle Mookie was miserable. He missed his old drinking buddies; he didn't have anything in common with "them ol' dope boys," as he would call them. Minnie, on the other hand, loved all the new activity. With her newfound wealth, she was living ghetto fabulous! She traded her old captain's chair for a shiny new leather one with pockets on the side that held up to twelve cans of beer. Minnie's fingers were laden with dirty little diamond rings that people had either sold or traded for crack. Now instead of four shiny gold teeth, she had five, one with a diamond in it! Minnie was happy and didn't care who wasn't happy around her.

On one particular Monday morning, Rose May was sleeping late because she and Libby had been on a smoke-a-thon all weekend. All of a sudden, Rose May's bedroom door swung open so violently it cracked the mirror on the wall. There stood Rose looming over her like big oak tree! All Rose May saw was Rose's angry twisted brow. She was down so close in her face, she could still smell the bacon, eggs, and coffee she'd had for breakfast. Rose snatched Rose May out of the bed by her collar.

"Ma! What you doing here?" Rose May asked, seeing double, trying to stall for time to think up a lie.

"No! The question is what the hell are you doing here? You supposed to have your dumb fast ass in school! Have you lost your mind?" Rose yelled while smacking Rose May upside her head repeatedly. Rose May had never seen her mother so furious! Rose continued, "I got a call from that school today. They said you haven't been in school in weeks, Rose May! Weeks!" Rose screamed.

Rose May just stood there looking foolish. She couldn't say a word. Her head hurt. Not just from all the crack she and Libby had smoked that weekend, but from the pummeling her mother had just put on her.head.

"I knew I shouldn't have taken that job out of town!" Rose shouted. Just as Rose took a deep breath to continue, Minnie stepped through the door, smelling of stale cigarettes and gin.

"Now you wait one damn minute, Rose!" Minnie slurred. "This be my damn house, and you ain't gone come in here with that damn shit! I been seeing after that gal all this time, and you ain't had nothing to say 'bout nothing! I ain't even charge you one damn dime!"

As Minnie attempted to continue, Rose yelled, "I knew what kind of house you ran Minnie, but I made sure you had sense enough to look after Rose May better than this! You know she needs to go to school! Have you lost yo damn mind too?" Rose was absolutely furious, and Minnie could see it. "I should call the police on yo dumb, ignorant black ass!" Rose threatened.

"Call the police?" Minnie yelled and asked at the same time. "You call the police, you might as well call the funeral home too 'cause if you bring to police here, I'm gon' kill yo ass!" Minnie exclaimed, reaching in her left bra cup.

Just then, Rose grabbed Minnie's wrist and threw her down on the dusty hardwood floor. Rose May was crouched in the corner, crying. She knew it was on now! Rose was an easygoing, kindhearted woman, but when you messed with her child, you messed with her.

"I know you ain't fixin' to cut me, bitch! I'll kill you dead right now!" Rose said while straddling Minnie, trying to retrieve the rusty blade Minnie was holding so tightly.

As Minnie struggled under Rose's kung fu grip, Uncle Mookie shot through the door.

"Rose! Rose! Get off her now! Y'all be kinfolk!" Mookie exclaimed while pulling Rose off of Minnie and securing the rusty blade.

"She ain't no kin of mine!" Minnie yelled, struggling to get up while twisting her wig back in place.

Rose began, "You a damn fool, Minnie, if you think Rose May can lay up here all day every day and do nothing!"

"She don't just be around here doing nothing," Mookie interjected while still holding Minnie tightly by her chubby bicep. "Rose, now, right is right and done told Minnie 'bout them ol' dope boys she let hang around here! That ol' New York, he the ringleader! That's who yo baby girl done took up wit'! Minnie ain't saying a damn thing 'cause she love a dollar!" Just then, Minnie shot Mookie a glance that would have killed him if it had been a dagger. Mookie continued, as if glad the gig was up. "I done told Minnie something bad was gon' happen if she keep letting them old no-good niggas hang around here and push they dope!" Mookie confessed.

Minnie had listened to all she could, "You shut yo damn mouth, Mookie!" Minnie hollered. "You be happy long as yo glass stay full!" Minnie said, fuming.

"Rose May, pack yo shit! You going home with me!" Rose stated, rolling her eyes hard at Minnie.

Rose began snatching up Rose May's things, throwing them on the bed. Rose May got up and did as she was told. Minnie, by this time, had allowed Mookie to drag her up to the front. She could still be heard though, calling Rose all kind of profane names. As Rose opened the closet door and began snatching clothes off the hangers, she knocked a box over, and gin bottles, cigarettes, crack pipes, chore boy, lighters, rolling papers, baggies, pushers, and weed residue tumbled to the floor. Rose May gasped in fear. As Rose stood there in utter disbelief, shaking her head, Minnie reappeared through the doorway. "Oh! You think you all high and mighty 'cause you workin' for them old rich white folks! You always did think you was above me...wit' yo long hair, good shape, and white folks' skin...you ain't no more than me, heffer! You the same dirty ho that got off that bus seventeen years ago!" Minnie spewed, ready to go another round.

"Minnie," Rose said, looking at her through squinted eyes and talking through her teeth, "if I wasn't a saved woman, I'd bust yo black ass right now!"

Uncle Mookie had to get between the two women to keep them from clashing again. Rose pushed his hand down, turned to Rose May, who was cramming things into a bag, and said, "Come on, fool! Get yo shit and let's go!" Rose May wasn't moving fast enough. "Right now! Before I lose my religion! That stuff in that box is from the devil, and you better leave it right here with the devil!" Rose yelled.

Upon exiting the disheveled room, Rose gave Minnie a look that could kill.

Minnie yelled, "Go on! I don't need you! You or yo crackhead-ass gal!" She then turned and looked accusingly at Rose May, who had tears streaming down her cheeks. "I know all about you smokin' that stuff! You think I don't know what you been doin'? Make like you just be drinkin'! I know! Peoples talk!" Minnie said with a wicked grin.

Rose May was hurt. She thought Aunt Minnie was her partner. All she could do was hang her head in shame and follow Rose out to the car. Rose turned to Rose May when they got in the car, obviously still very angry, and said, "I know you ain't gone and got yourself on drugs, have you?"

Rose May didn't answer.

"Have you?" Rose screamed, followed by a slap that stung like a bee, a few bees.

"No mam…I swear I ain't." Rose May lied.

"I trusted Minnie to look after you! I should have known better!" Rose said as she dug off in a cloud of smoke.

This wasn't the only smoke that would be in the Carlisle women's lives.

10

A few weeks had gone by since the big fight at Aunt Minnie's house. Rose was working hard but not as hard as before, and never out of town. She knew she needed to be around more to get Rose May on the right track.

Rose May hadn't had a drink, smoked, or snorted anything since she was dragged from Aunt Minnie's house, but she wanted to. Sometimes, the urge would get so unbearable she could hardly stand it. Furthermore, she hadn't even seen or heard from Bobby. She did hear through the grapevine that business was booming over at Aunt Minnie's spot.

"Rose May, I'm going to work now, and I don't want any foolishness while I'm gone. You better not have anybody in here, and you better not go out!" Rose said, gathering up her purse, coat, and keys. "You hear me, girl?" Rose said.

"Yes, mam, Momma," Rose May solemnly replied.

Rose felt that everything was on track now that Rose May was back home and in school. But little did she know.

It was only a matter of time before the ugly crack demon would rear its head, with seven more attached.

Rose May was fixing herself a sandwich when she heard a knock at the door.

"Who is it?" Rose May asked excitedly.

"It's Tony," the voice on the other side of the door replied.

Rose May wasn't thrilled, but she was happy for any type of action. Rose May opened the door with sandwich in hand. "Hey, Tony, what's up?" she asked, letting Tony and his wide grin through the door.

"You!" Tony replied, leaning forward for a kiss, only to get dismissed. "I heard what happened at Aunt Minnie's house. I'm glad you are out of there," Tony said, plopping on the couch.

Rose May was really agitated. She wanted to get high, and Tony and his mouth weren't helping the situation. Tony continued as Rose May just sat there eating her sandwich, while watching an episode of *Dallas* on TV.

"New York and his boys got it on lock over there at Minnie's place. People be up in there smoking crack and everything!" Tony rattled on. "Minnie and Mookie be fighting all the time. They be drunk 24-7!" Tony stated emphatically. Tony rattled on so fast he almost ran out of breath. He was just ecstatic to be in Rose May's presence. "I'm glad you left that sorry nigga New York alone. I told you he was no good," Tony said, sliding closer to Rose May on the couch.

"I didn't leave him alone," Rose May said pitifully. "He left me alone."

"Good," said Tony, "because I heard you had started smoking." Tony inquired in a very caring tone, "You ain't smoking no more, are you?"

"No," said Rose May. "It wasn't as bad as everybody made it out to be."

"Well, I'm just glad you home with yo mamma." It was obvious that he meant it by the passionate way he looked at Rose May.

"Tony, you gotta go," Rose May said, getting up, hoping he would follow her to the door. "I ain't supposed to have nobody here when my momma ain't here."

"All right, all right, I'm going. I just came by to check on you. Don't yo momma like that no more," Tony said, with Rose May practically pushing him out the door. "Call me. You know you gon' always be my girl no matter what!"

"Bye, Tony," Rose May said, becoming noticeably disturbed as she slammed the door behind him.

Rose May slammed the door on Tony, but not on her mind.

11

All Rose May could think about was what was going on at Aunt Minnie's. She wanted to be there, not just in her mind! Rose May looked at the clock, it was only 10:00 p.m. She knew her mother wouldn't get off until seven in the morning. She had plenty of time. She would just go around the corner, get one rock, just one, and then come home.

When Rose May returned home, it was eight o'clock in the morning. Rose was home, and boy, was she mad!

"Where you been, girl?" Rose asked in an unusually high pitch.

Rose May couldn't say a thing; all she could do was stand there, looking dumbfounded.

"You hear me talking to you, girl?" Rose screamed.

The next thing Rose May felt was a hard slap across her face.

"Don't you ever, long as you live, stay out of my house all night! I told you not to go nowhere!" By now, Rose was screaming at the top of her lungs. "Where you been? It don't take all night to do nothing! I hope you ain't been laying up with some sorry ass man! Giiirl, you gone kill me!" Rose huffed as she sat down on the bottom of Rose May's bed and let out a big sigh.

"Ma, it won't happen again. I promise. I'm sorry," Rose May said sorrowfully.

She was so convincing Rose believed her. "Now get dressed!" Rose ordered. "You going to school, and you gon' graduate! You got a half year left, and you gon' graduate if it kills me!" Rose strongly stated.

Rose didn't realize that it wasn't a man Rose May was laying up with, it was a glass pipe.

12

"Rose May, Rose May? You at home?" Rose knew as she called her daughter's name, in her deepest heart of hearts, she knew she would not get an answer. She was exhausted, not only from working long hard hours at the hospital, but from trying to keep up with Rose May and her now full-blown crack addiction.

Rose May was eighteen now and had quit school. Rose felt like she could do nothing but pray. After all, she hardly ever saw Rose May anymore. The only time she came home was to change clothes or manipulate her out of some money. Most of the time, she had no problem because Rose was so glad to see her Rose May could get anything she had. Rose May was so good at manipulating her mother until most of the time, Rose didn't know it had happened until Rose May was long gone. Rose was so disappointed that Rose May hadn't finished high school. She had heard all the talk about the people Rose May was hanging out with and the things she was doing to support her habit. She refused to believe any of it—not the beautiful, outgoing, fun-loving daughter she had. She just wouldn't believe any of it. She still had high hopes for Rose May.

Rose knew her daughter was hanging around Minnie's all the time, and she knew why. That no-good-for-nothing dope-dealing boyfriend of hers, New York, he was just using her. Why couldn't she see that? Rose prayed day in and day out that there would be a change. She wanted her daughter saved! There was no sense talking to her; they would just end up in a heated argument that sometimes came to blows. Rose just worked, went to church, and prayed. She often thought of going over to Minnie's and dragging her daughter out of that hellhole or even calling the police. She just didn't know what to do. Rose reached in her handbag and pulled out a red book one of her coworkers had given her. The cover read PRAYERS. Rose flipped through the pages halfheartedly until she came to a prayer that said "Prayer for a lost loved one". Rose looked up at the ceiling, fell on her knees, and began to pray for her poor, lost, stupid girl.

13

It was Friday night, and Minnie's spot was jumping. Not only was it Friday night; it was the first of the month! As Mookie turned the corner to go home, he could hear the music, smell the fish frying, and most of all, he thought, *Them damn dope boys!*

As bad as Mookie wanted a drink of gin and a good hot fish sandwich, he just couldn't take all the chaos anymore. Instead of making a left at the corner, he made a right and walked a ways down the block. As he approached Mt. Jubilee Missionary Baptist Church, he heard the sweetest-sounding voices he had ever heard. It was as if Mookie was in a trance as he opened the door, walked past the usher, and sat on the last pew. Mookie watched the preacher as he practically begged the audience to give their lives to Christ.

As he gazed intently at the wooden cross that hung over the pulpit, his life flashed before him. He thought about the rugged life he'd had growing up dirt poor in the sticks of Alabama. Mookie and his brothers were shipped off to relatives after his parents were killed in a bad car accident.

Mookie grew up under the tutelage of a drunken uncle and a God-fearing aunt. He knew about the Lord but never really paid much attention until now. He could always remember his Aunt Ella Ruth saying, "The Lawd'll make a way out uh no way. Malachi, you just put yo trust in the Good Master, and He'll make sho' you gets yo name in that Lamb's Book of Life!"

As Mookie came back in focus, and he heard the choir singing "Amazing Grace," he knew that it was time to make that change. He felt it in the pit of his stomach. Mookie stood up, stepped out in the aisle, and began his descent to the altar. When Mookie reached the altar, tears of joy were streaming down his face because he knew this day his name would be written in the Lamb's Book of Life.

14

"Rose May, sit yo ass down somewhere!" New York said as he was bagging up what looked like a hundred-twenty-dollar sacks of dope. "Girl, I told you not to smoke too much of that shit!" he said agitatedly. "It's some fire! You know I gotta pay Big Red before the night is out, and he ain't playing!" New York was furious! "Pass me that bag of powder! I wanna get high too," New York said, grabbing the bag from the table.

Rose May was high out of her mind. She was peeping out windows, opening doors, digging on the floor, and everything else. Not only was she high, Aunt Minnie was up front, falling down drunk, cursing everybody out.

New York was getting skied up and was a little nervous. "Lock that door! And sit yo ass down, Rose May! You making me nervous! Go see who up front!" New York yelled while fidgeting with everything in front of him. "I gotta get this paper straight, and you ain't making it easy!" he yelled even louder.

Rose May tried to get up, but she was stuck. Dope was everywhere! It was too much commotion going on up front. New York grabbed his gat. Rose May was too high to even notice that he had his finger on the trigger. Just then, Minnie burst through the door with a glass in her hand. New York twirled around, lifted the gun, and pulled the trigger. *Bang!* New York had shot Aunt Minnie in the head!

Rose May jumped up, screaming, "Aunt Minnie, Aunt Minnie!"

Blood was everywhere!

"I told you to lock that damn door!" New York said hysterically. As he stood there not believing what had just happened, he grabbed his head and spun around and around; sheer pandemonium set in.

All you could hear were glasses dropping, tables turning over, doors slamming, and feet scuffling. The only thing left at Aunt Minnie's were empty turned over glasses, ashtrays still smoking, hot grease still popping, bags of dope, lighters, drug paraphernalia, empty and full bottles of gin, cans of opened and unopened beer, and one mean, dirty old dead woman who lived a mean, dirty life.

As soon as Rose hit the corner coming from work, she saw all the police cars and ambulances at Minnie's. Her heart sank, and her eyes began to well up with tears. All she could think was Rose May, Rose May, Rose May. Rose pulled up, got out of the car, and began to walk cautiously toward the crowd. She heard Mookie crying and saying, "I told Minnie something bad was gon' happen! I told her! Now she done gone…my poor Minnie done left here with a bullet to her head! Lawd, Lawd, Lawd!" Mookie yelled.

Rose was in shock. She had not seen or spoken to Minnie since their fight.

"Lord, I feel awful! Please forgive me! I should have known better! I'm a Christian. Minnie didn't know no better!" Rose said sorrowfully.

Looking up, she saw New York being led away in handcuffs by the police.

"Where's Rose May, boy! Where she at?" Rose shouted.

The boy was in a daze, and he didn't even look her way. Rose went home as fast as she could. There she found Rose May crouched in a corner, crying uncontrollably.

"Rose May, baby you all right?" she asked with concern in her voice.

All Rose May could do was look up sorrowfully at her mother and cry. "I saw it all, Momma. I saw it all!" She wept. "Poor Aunt Minnie gone, and it's all my fault!"

"It ain't yo fault, child. You, better than anybody, knew the lifestyle Minnie led," Rose said.

"I know, Momma, I never should've started going with New York! He never would've been there!" Rose May cried on.

"Hush, child, the good Lord knows what He doing. I been praying for a change, and a change done come. I feel bad for Minnie 'cause we was close at one time, real close.

But God don't like ugly, and Minnie had some ugly ways!" Rose rattled on. "I just hope you learned something from this. God saved you, Rose May. That could have been you!" Rose stopped, thought a minute, then started again, "It's time to make a change, baby, and I'll be there with you every step of the way!" She stopped then added, "Along with the Lord, you know."

15

Rose May did make a change after Aunt Minnie's death. She went to school, got her GED, and enrolled in a technical college to train for a nursing degree. Rose was so proud. She was glad to see her daughter had straightened up. She was even going to church with her mom occasionally.

Rose May was extremely beautiful; she never had a problem attracting men. She had just turned twenty-one and had about three more years before she would finish her nursing degree. Things seemed to be great on the outside, but on the inside Rose May was a mess! She had stopped using crack since Aunt Minnie's death, but she hadn't stopped drinking and partying. Rose had stopped working so many hours so that she would be able to spend more time at home. She was beginning to realize what her absence had done to Rose May, and she wanted to make it up to her if she could.

She noticed Rose May with different men all the time, but as Rose May explained to her mother, "They're just friends, Ma." She failed to mention they were friends with benefits. Rose gladly accepted the skimpy explanations because she loved her daughter so much and was glad to see her making something of herself. Rose didn't even say anything when she smelled a faint whiff of gin on her breath every now and then. Little did Rose know these weren't just friends; they were tricks! Rose May loved nice things and money. She picked that spirit up from Aunt Minnie. She also had Aunt Minnie's philosophy about men: "Money, honey, that's all I want!"

Rose was clearly in denial. Where did she think Rose May was getting all of these fine clothes, shoes, and jewelry? She always had money in her pocket. Rose didn't care as long as Rose May spent a little time with her and went to church with her every now and then. She didn't even realize that Rose May was like a dam ready to burst!

16

It was Friday night, and Mount Jubilee Missionary Baptist Church was having revival all week long.

Rose May was getting all gussied up because she had a date to meet at nine. Boy, was she wearing that red dress! Rose May had a figure like an hour glass and beautiful long hair with auburn streaks. There was no denying it. Rose May was fine, and she knew it!

Rose May entered the door as Rose was getting ready. "Girl, you know you looking good and smelling good too! That smells like some expensive perfume. One of those friends of yours give it to you?" Rose said sarcastically.

"Aww, Momma, don't start," Rose May snapped. "You know I like to look good and smell good too, and I love myself some shoes!" Rose May said braggadociously.

"I wanted you to go to church with me tonight, Rose May. They got this powerful man of God running revival this week, and they say he's good. Please come and go with me tonight," Rose pleaded. "Go with me this one night, and I won't ask you no more this week," Rose insisted.

"Ma, come on, I'll go next time!" Rose May said obnoxiously.

"Rose May, I do all I can to help you, and you can't do this one thing for the only mother you'll have?" Rose begged.

Rose May felt guilty, so she reluctantly agreed. Rose was elated!

"I'm going, Momma, but as soon as they pass the plate I'm leaving to go on my date." It sounded so disrespectful she hurriedly added, "Okay?"

"Okay!" Rose said as she almost skipped to her room to get dressed.

Rose May did feel obligated to go because her mother did quite a bit to help her, and she hadn't been all up in her business, so that made it easier to turn her tricks.

Rose May knew that her mother loved her dearly and worshiped the very ground on which she walked. As she turned around to take another look in the mirror, she gasped! What she saw as her reflection was a hideous monster! She sat on the bed and began to weep. Just then, Rose walked in the room.

"What's wrong, baby? I thought you were ready," Rose said curiously.

Rose May sobbed as she fell into her mother's arms. "I look so ugly and fat! I see a monster in the mirror, Ma!" She sobbed.

"Chiiild, please!" Rose said. "You're the prettiest thing this side of the Mason–Dixon line! Everybody always talking about you and what a fine-looking young woman you are. You must be crazy! Now get yourself up, dry up those tears, and let's go hear what the good Reverend Jerimiah Jones got to say 'bout the Lord!" Rose exclaimed very excitedly.

As Rose and her daughter entered the church, everyone turned to look at them as they were a bit late. They both looked stunning. They actually looked like sisters.

"Ma," Rose May whispered, "why we gotta go all the way up to the front?"

Rose kept walking. "Hush, girl, and come on," Rose said quietly through her teeth as she proudly walked up to the front pew and sat down.

Rose was so elated that her daughter was there beside her. Rose May sat there quietly slouched in the pew looking unconcerned, until a nicely dressed man that was the color of a Hershey Bar entered through the side door and sat in the pulpit. Rose May immediately perked up. She thought to herself, *Ooooooh, ooooooh, he know he fine!* His hair was smooth and shiny like black velvet. His lips were full and plump, and he had a set of the prettiest white straight teeth she had ever seen. She felt like getting up saying Hallelujiah! He even had a cute little dimple on the side of his cheek.

"Ma, I know that ain't the preacher, is it?" Rose May asked, leaning over to whisper.

"Hush, girl! Stop lusting in the house of the Lord!" Rose said, pinching Rose May on the thigh.

As the choir sang, Rose May didn't hear a thing they sang. She couldn't keep her eyes of the "Hershey Bar." When the choir finished, the Hershey Bar was introduced. "And now we will receive the Word of God from Reverend Jerimiah Jones, all the way from New York City."

As the good reverend began to deliver the message, Rose May was mesmerized at how eloquently he spoke. His northern accent enchanted her. Rose May was amening more than the amen corner. Rose was so happy; she really thought Rose May was receiving the Word. The Word was not what Rose May was thinking about receiving.

When the service ended, Rose May was still there. Rose took her by the hand and led her to meet the man of God. They struggled through the sea of churchgoers. "Reverend Jones, that was a good message, a good message. This is my daughter, Rose May."

"Pleased to meet you," the reverend said, shaking Rose May's hand.

Rose May looked into his coal black eyes and knew the look oh so well. "Very, very pleased to meet you too, Reverend Jones."

"Maybe we can have you over for dinner before you leave," Rose interjected.

"It would be my pleasure. I don't know when I've had a good home cooked meal," the reverend replied.

"My momma makes the best fried chicken and lemonade around here," Rose May said.

As Rose May and her mother turned to leave, Rose May could feel his eyes on her. On the ride home, she was full of questions about the good Reverend Jerimiah Jones.

"How long he gone be here, Ma? Is he married? How old is he?" Rose May asked, bombing her mother with questions.

"Slow down, girl, that ain't one of those 'friends' you asking about. That's a man of God! And if you got any sense in your foolish head, you'll try to learn something from him! Maybe he can give you some counseling or something to get you on the right track of life. I'm gone ask him to dinner tomorrow." Rose planned.

"Good," Rose May said, "I could probably use some good counseling right about now."

Saturday night couldn't come quick enough for Rose May. Rose had invited Reverend Hershey Bar for dinner.

Rose May was scurrying around looking for something to wear, while Rose was finishing her batch of finger-licking good fried chicken. Rose May came out in one of the shortest, tightest low-cut dresses she had.

"Negro! You better get yo fast ass back in that room and find something to cover it up! This is a damn preacher, Rose May! You can't be trying to tempt the man of God! He'll think you some kind of Jezebel or something!" Rose scolded.

Rose May sucked her teeth and went back to find something more churchie to put on. She put on a long brown dress with a severely high neckline. The brown potato-sack dress still showed her shapely figure; it couldn't be helped. Even with her hair pulled back and no makeup on, she was still breathtaking.

At seven sharp, the doorbell rang. Rose May jumped up quickly to answer the door.

"I'll get it! You just sit it on down, missy!" Rose said.

After Rose opened the door, she said, "Come on in, Reverend Jones, you right on time. I got a good hot meal waiting on you." Rose asked, "You remember my daughter, Rose May, don't you?"

"Yes, yes, I do," replied the reverend. "It's a pleasure again. I see where she gets her beauty." Both women blushed.

Rose May was absolutely speechless! This was the prettiest blackest man she had ever seen; and she had seen a good many men. As they sat down to dinner, and Rose May poured the lemonade in the glass, she leaned over the reverend and got a whiff of some of the best-smelling cologne she had ever smelled. She saw him cut his eye to look at her cleavage that wasn't there because her mother made her cover it up with this ugly potato-sack dress!

They all ate and made small talk. Rose May began to feel very comfortable talking to the reverend. He asked her questions about her life and what standing she was in with the Lord, and she asked him questions about his life. Some of her questions were followed by a kick under the table from Rose. Rose May watched closely as the reverend took a bite out of his fried chicken. She couldn't help but think, *I wish I was a piece of fried chicken right now*, and the grease from the chicken made his lips even more luscious.

"Rose May? Rose May? Did you hear what Reverend Jones said?" Rose asked.

"Uh, no, Ma, I'm sorry, what?" Rose May said, snapping out of her fried chicken fantasy.

"Reverend Jones said he'll be here for about three weeks, and you can go over to the church for some counseling, and he can teach you about what it means to be saved," Rose stated very hopeful.

"How does that sound Rose May?" Reverend Jones interjected.

"Fine. Just fine, Ma," Rose May answered dreamily. "When and what time? I really, really want to be saved," Rose May said mockingly.

"How about Monday afternoon around three?" Reverend Jones asked.

"Sounds great to me, Reverend Jones," Rose May said, smiling showing off her deep dimples.

Rose was elated. She really thought Rose May was serious about getting saved. The only thing Rose May was serious about was getting laid.

Monday came, and Rose May was watching the clock. She purposely didn't go to church on Sunday so

Reverend Jones would anticipate seeing her, and on top of that, she partied really hard Saturday night and had a massive hangover.

Rose hadn't gotten home from work yet, so she didn't have to worry about dressing churchie. Rose May put on a tight red sweater that showed her perfectly shaped bosom with just a hint of cleavage. She wiggled into a pair of Sergio Valente jeans that fit like a glove, slipped on her red ankle boots, splashed on some Chanel N°5, took four shots of gin, and was out the door for her counseling session with the good reverend.

Rose May was looking fine as she strolled hard down the avenue. Heads were turning and horns were blowing. *Boy, am I missing some good money!* Rose May thought as she freshened up her lipstick. *He better be doing some damn good counseling!* Her mind flipped. Right now, Rose May had one thing on her mind, well make that two things on her mind: Reverend Jones and where they would end up tonight!

Rose May got to the church about ten minutes to three. Reverend Jones was already in place. As she walked through the door and closed it behind her, he grabbed her up instantly.

"Girl, I been thinking about you all day long and watching the clock," Reverend Jones said lustfully.

"What you doing?" Rose May cried.

"Don't play with me, girl! You know exactly what I'm doing! I saw you the moment I stepped in the pulpit!" the "good reverend" said, blowing his hot sweet breath across her face.

Rose May was swept off her feet as he pulled her tightly around her waist and kissed her softly on the neck.

"Sugar, you know you smell good…Chanel N°5?" he asked seductively.

Rose May nodded her head up and down.

"That's my favorite!" Reverend Jones said in a sexy tone.

Rose May was in shock. She never expected this! She thought she would have to be the aggressor, but it was just the opposite. This really turned her on! *But wait!* she thought, *he was supposed to be a man of God!* Rose May was both confused and turned on at the same time.

"I've got to have you, Rose May!" Reverend Jones said as he moved his hands from her waist to her hips. "I've never felt this way about a woman before," he said, breathing heavily.

Now Rose May was really confused! She didn't know whether to think about love, lust, or money! It felt so good to have a man hold her tight and whisper sweet things in her ear. Rose May was like a puppet, and he was the puppeteer.

"Let's get out of here and go someplace a little cozier, okay?" The mesmerizing Jeremiah Jones cooed in her ear.

As they rode in his big shiny black Cadillac to the Shady Oak Motel, Reverend Jones was holding her hand, telling her how beautiful she was, and how easy it would be for a man to fall in love with her. When Rose May looked at him and saw the word *love* come through his beautiful lips, her heart skipped a beat. Rose May's mind was all messed up. Reverend Jones wasn't like her regular friends with benefits. He felt like the one! Could she possibly be in love already? She'd heard of love at first sight before, but she never believed in it. But after her passionate night at the Shady Oak Motel, she knew she was in love!

17

Rose May made it in just before Rose came home. Rose had worked a double that night, and as soon as Rose May hit the sheets, her door swung open.

"How was your counseling session with Reverend Jones?" Rose asked clearly excited.

Rose May rolled over as if she had been in a deep sleep, still smelling like the Hugo Boss cologne Reverend Jones was wearing.

"Oh hey, Ma," she said, pretending to be groggy. "It was good. We talked and went out for coffee." Rose May lied, trying not to show her true emotions.

"He sure is a fine gentleman, ain't he?" Rose continued, trying to strike up a conversation.

Yeeeeees Looooord! Rose May said in her mind, but to her mother, she answered a very unconcerned, "He's all right."

"I'm just glad you got somebody who knows what he's talking about and can tell you how to get to those Pearly Gates. Yes sir! A fine God-fearing man ready to be of good service for the Master," Rose said as he closed her daughter's door and walked off humming the old familiar hymn, "Amazing grace how sweet the sound that saved a wretch like me."

Rose May was saying amazing too, but not amazing grace. Rose May was foolish enough to think that she was really in love. She was so confused. She had never felt anything that felt like this with a man before. Aunt Minnie sure didn't tell her anything about this side of a man, and neither did Rose. She didn't know if it was love or not, but she was going to ride this good, good feeling for as long as she could. As a she matter of fact, she had a "counseling session" tonight she could hardly wait! Good thing she was on spring break, she had much more free time to be "counseled."

The phone rang about noon. Rose May heard her mother say, "Hey, Reverend Jones, how are you? I'm so glad you're taking up some of your valuable time to help get Rose May get saved and on the right track. I sure do appreciate you." Rose rattled on, "Okay, Reverend, hold on. I'll get her." Rose yelled directly in the receiver, "Rooose Maaay, telephone. It's the reverend."

On Rose's call, Rose May almost fell as she popped out of the bed, becoming entangled in the covers. The two women anxiously met and exchanged the phone receiver. It was hard to tell who was most excited.

"Hi, Reverend Jones," Rose May said dreamily. "How are you?" she asked as she snapped back into reality.

"Fine, just fine," he replied in a raspy, sexy voice. "I'll be even better when I can hold my sweet baby doll tonight. I can't get you off my mind!"

"Ah, yes I will," Rose May said, attempting to talk in code. "Sure I'll be there about four, and we can go over those scriptures so I can get a clearer understanding," Rose May said sheepishly. "Okay, bye," she abruptly ended the conversation when Rose walked by her.

"What scriptures are you going over? Maybe I can study them with you," Rose said very excited.

"Aw, Ma it's kind of personal," Rose May said softly.

"Oh, okay, I understand. I'm just glad you are in the Good Book," she chuckled.

Four o'clock came, and Rose May was in room 622 at the Shady Oak Motel with Pink Champale chilling on ice, waiting for Reverend Jones to arrive. Rose May lit a cigarette. Just then, the door opened. Reverend Jones stepped over the threshold and quickly closed the door behind him. "Come here my, baby doll! You are something to see! Good Lord! Come, give daddy some of that sweet brown sugar!" He growled, proceeding to undress Rose May with his sexy bedroom eyes.

Rose May was in a daze. She was like a robot. As she leaned into Reverend Jones and smelled his sweet pepperminty breath, felt his soft silky chocolate skin, and felt his strong powerful hands caress her, she felt like she was in heaven. This was only their second night together, but Rose May felt like she could be with this man forever. After they made love over and over again, he held her in his arms, and they talked for what seemed like hours. They talked about everything!

She confided in him about everything she could think of and told him her deepest secrets. She felt so safe and secure in his arms. It felt too good to be true! Rose May was blind, crazy in love! So blind and crazy she couldn't see the pit of hell she was falling into.

18

Reverend Jones was preaching Wednesday night at Mount Nebo Missionary Baptist Church, and Rose May had already picked out what she was wearing. Her mother was so happy to see her taking such an interest in church.

"Rose May," Rose yelled down the hall, "I know you going to hear Reverend Jones preach tonight, ain't you?"

"Yeah, Ma," Rose May replied, looking up at the ceiling.

"I sure hate I gotta work a double tonight. I need some Word in my spirit. I know he gone be good," Rose said, ironing her uniform.

"He sure is going to be good," Rose May chuckled under her breath.

"What you say?" Rose hollered.

"Nothing, Momma. I said I'm sure he will be good. I'll tell you about it in the morning," Rose May said with a devilish grin.

"Okay, baby. I sure am glad to know you'll be here when I get home. Now I can work in some peace." Rose let out a sigh when she reflected on Rose May's turbulent past.

Just as Rose left for work, the phone rang. It was the good reverend.

"Hello," Rose May answered in an upbeat tone.

"Hey, baby doll," Reverend Jones answered hesitantly. "Is your mother home?"

"No, she's gone to work," Rose May replied.

"Good. I thought she might have answered the phone," he said in a more comfortable tone.

"She hates she won't be there to hear you tonight. She'll be there tomorrow," Rose May said jubilantly.

"Well then, how's my sweet baby doll doing this fine night?" he said, switching to mack mode.

"Just fine now," Rose May answered smiling coyly on the on the other end of the phone.

"Listen, baby," Reverend Jones continued, "I just called to tell you not to come tonight because I won't be able to keep my eyes off you while I'm in the pulpit, and I need to be focused on the Lord."

"What?" Rose May whined. "I already had my clothes laid out and everything."

He could hear the disappointment in her voice and quickly said, "Hold on, baby doll. That doesn't mean I don't want to see you." He continued to explain, "You be ready and waiting for me at our spot. I won't make one stop until

I get to those rosy red lips of yours. Oh yeah, wear that sexy red teddy I bought you with those hot red pumps."

There was a pause, then he said, "You hear me, baby doll?"

Rose May's smile lit up like a Christmas tree as she said softly and sexily, "Okay, big daddy, I'll be ready and waiting."

Rose May didn't realize she was waiting on a man that would change the course of her life forever!

19

Rose May got to the Shady Oak about nine o'clock. She figured church would be out around ten or so, and she wanted everything to be perfect. She took a nice hot bubble bath, bathed down in her Chanel N°5, put on her sexy red teddy with her hot red pumps, put the champagne on ice (she had a bottle or two of gin in her purse for herself), smoked two and a half joints, popped in her Anita Baker cassette, and waited on the man she thought she loved. She had no doubt he would be there because, boy, did she put it on him! He acted as though he couldn't get enough of her; not just her body, he said. He enjoyed her conversation and witty sense of humor.

"Could he really be the one?" she said to herself as she put her gin bottle to her lips, threw her head back, and killed half the bottle. When she saw the headlights of his Cadillac through the flimsy curtains, she got goose bumps. She could hardly wait for him to come through the door. He had a key, so he let himself in.

"There's my baby doll," he exclaimed as Rose May rushed into his arms, and he showered her with kisses.

He kissed her long and passionately. Rose May didn't know if her head was spinning from the gin, the weed, or the kiss. She picked all of the above. She felt good and loved. She was in love. After they made passionate love over and over again that night, he whispered the three words Rose May had so longed to hear, "I love you, baby doll."

Rose May was so happy to hear those three words, she thought she was floating. As daybreak approached, Rose May knew she had better get home before Rose. She didn't want to mess up this good thing by pissing Rose off. She attempted to slide out of the bed only to be pulled back in by the sexy preacher.

"Where you going, baby?" he asked, clearly aroused.

"I gotta get home before Momma does. She'll have a fit if she finds this out!" Rose May exclaimed.

"Spend the day with me, Rose May. I'll call your Momma and tell her I need you to go over to Kinley with me this morning, and we'll be gone all day. Maybe all night," he said, pulling Rose May tighter.

"Are you sure about that, JJ?" Rose May asked.

JJ is what she called him now that they were an item. (Only behind closed doors.)

"Yeah, baby doll, I'll call her. She trusts me," he said, reaching for the phone on the nightstand.

As promised, Reverend Jones called Rose who was quite hysterical by now because Rose May wasn't at home. Rose May looked on as the good reverend laid the lie out so smoothly.

"Hey, Sister Carlisle, this is Reverend Jones. I just wanted you to know that I picked Rose May up early this morning to ride over to Kinley to take care of some church business with me." He lied.

"Oh, thank God!" Rose cried. "I was worried and mad at the same time! I'm so glad you can use her to build up the Kingdom. I know she's in good hands with you," Rose said confidently.

"Well, don't you worry about a thing, Sister Rose, I'll have her home in a day or two." The reverend lied.

"Okay, Reverend Jones, let me speak to Rose May," Rose asked politely.

The slick-talking preacher handed Rose May the phone with an impish grin.

"Hey, Ma," Rose May said, feeling a little uneasy. She knew Rose could smell a rat if she sniffed long enough.

"You mind your manners and don't go over there making me shame! It's a privilege for Reverend Jones to be taking you!" Rose scolded.

"Okay, Ma, I'll see you soon," Rose May replied hanging up, trying to hurry off the phone because she was ashamed.

"See! What did I tell you? I got you, baby doll," the slickmouthed preacher said persuasively.

Rose May was more than happy to spend more time with JJ; but something deep, deep down in her soul just didn't feel right. She picked up her gin bottle, took a big swig, ignored the feeling, and focused on the love she was feeling.

Rose was singing a song when Rose May entered the door after supposedly being in Kinley with Reverend Jones.

"Hey, baby," Rose said. "Did you and Reverend Jones have a good time in Kinley?" Rose inquired.

"Yeah, Ma, I guess so," Rose May solemnly answered.

"What do you mean you guess so? You didn't go up there and show out, did you?"

"No, Ma, why you always think I'm doing something crazy?" Rose May snapped.

"Well tell me about it. What scriptures and what kind of paperwork did he need you to help do?"

"Ma, I'm tired right now. We'll talk later," Rose May said as she went in her room and sat to sulk on her bed.

Rose May wasn't feeling right. She felt like she had a hole in her stomach. She just had an uneasy feeling. Even though she felt like she was in love, was love supposed to feel like this? Something just wasn't right. She suddenly had the urge to get high. She wanted some crack, and she wanted it right now! Her stomach was churning, and her head was pounding. Rose May quickly changed clothes and put on tennis shoes and a sweat suit. She zipped past her mother so fast Rose didn't have time to question her about where she was going.

"Rose May, where you goi…"—*slam!* Rose May was out the door.

Oh well, maybe she had some unfinished business with the preacher, Rose thought to herself.

With that, she continued happily and contently humming and cleaning.

Rose May had left the house about three o'clock that afternoon. It was now 10:00 p.m., and Rose hadn't heard a thing from her. Even Reverend Jones called to inquire of her whereabouts.

"I don't know where she is, Reverend Jones," Rose said in a trembling voice. "I haven't seen her since you dropped her off this afternoon. Did everything go okay in Kinley? Was she upset? Was anything bothering her?" Rose asked, bombarding the good reverend with question after question.

"Don't worry, Sister Rose. I'm sure she'll be home soon. I know she wouldn't want to miss any of our counseling sessions. I'll call you when I hear from her," the slick-mouthed preacher assured her before hanging up the phone.

As Rose hung up the phone, she had a sinking feeling in her gut that she hadn't felt for a long time. Rose trusted Reverend Jones at this point, but she felt like something just wasn't right. She knew her girl. In the back of her mind, she knew Rose May had gone to get some dope. She had seen that look in her eyes, but not for a long time. Rose just didn't want to believe that! Rose fell on her knees and began to pray, "Father, in the name of Jesus, you know where's my baby at. Keep her, Lord. Don't let her be back on them drugs. Keep her, Lord, she's the only one I got. Please, Jesus, keep her safe wherever she is!"

Just as Rose ended her prayer, the phone rang. "Hello!" Rose answered anxiously, hoping Rose May was on the other end.

"Hey, Ma," Rose May said.

"Giiiirrrrrl! Where the hell you at? You had me worried to death!"

"I had to get away for a while."

"You ain't smoking dope, are you?"

"No, Ma, I'm just over at a friends."

"Reverend Jones called too. When you coming home?"

"I'll be there in a little while."

"What's a little while, Rose May? Don't tell me no lie! Don't tell me you coming, and I won't see you for days!"

"I'll be home, Ma, I promise." Rose May just hung up the phone and continued smoking.

After the clock struck midnight, Rose knew she wouldn't be seeing Rose May this night. She knew and there was no denying it, Rose May was smoking crack and there was no telling when she would see her.

Rose called in to work the next day she couldn't go. She just sat anxiously by the phone and waited, and waited, and waited. Finally, the phone rang! Rose picked up on half a ring.

"Hello!" Rose answered breathlessly. "Oh, hey, Reverend Jones," Rose said disappointedly, "I thought you were Rose May."

"Oh, she's here with me, I told you everything would be all right," the good reverend said.

"Is she all right? Where has she been? Let me speak to her!" Rose said, changing from sad to mad.

"She's fine, just fine. She just fell by the wayside and backslid a little. She'll be just fine. She doesn't want to come home right now. I'll take her to get something to eat, talk to her, and then I'll take her by my Aunt Charlotte's house to get cleaned up. Then we'll all pray and see what the Good Lord has to say about the matter," the sly pastor said.

"Okay, Reverend Jones," Rose said, feeling reassured. "I can rest much better knowing that she's with you and under your care."

Rose hung up the phone and rubbed her stomach. She had a bad feeling in the pit of her belly. She just shook it off, decided to go take a good hot bath, and go to bed. She felt like she had been out doing crack all night. Little did she know her baby girl was in the clutches of Satan's grip that very moment.

20

As Rose May sat on the bed next to Reverend Jones, she felt absolutely awful! He tried to comfort her as she sobbed uncontrollably.

"Come on, baby doll, try to pull yourself together. It's going to be all right. I've talked to your mother, and she's fine, and you're here safe with me. Everybody can make a little slip sometimes but see that's what's good about God. All you have to do is ask Him to forgive you, and it's thrown in the sea of forgetfulness," he said reassuringly.

Rose May flashed him a look like she was going to cut him. "Oh, that's what you do every time you lay up with me, tell me you love me, and then drop me off at my momma's house? Do you really love me? Because I don't believe love will make me want to go out and smoke crack!" Rose May yelled.

"Rose May, baby, calm down. You know I care about you deeply, and I'm very concerned about your well-being, and I'm not ever going to let anything happen to you," he said very convincingly.

"But do you love me? Really love me?" Rose May asked.

"Of course I do. I love all God's children," he replied.

Rose May was about to snap! "You slick talking black son of a bitch! You know what I mean!"

"Rose May, you know I have certain obligations I have to fulfill in New York and some loose ends I need to tie up."

"What the hell do you mean loose ends? Nigga, I know you ain't married. You ain't been wearing no ring, and you sure ain't been acting like a married man! You been acting like it's all about me! You just told me the other night that you loved me! Now we need to get this shit straight and get it straight right now! Do we or do we not have a future together?"

The good reverend was getting a little uneasy, so he figured he'd better start running some game.

"Baby doll, of course, we'll be together. And yes, we have a future. Do you think I'd let a fine woman like you get away? Like I said, baby, I just got some loose ends to tie up upstate, and I'll send for you. So just ease up and let's enjoy the time we have left together."

Rose May just melted in his arms when she heard his consoling words. She so wanted to believe what he was saying. But why did she still feel that hole in her stomach?

"Now let me run you a hot bath, so you can relax, and I can hold you, and you can tell big daddy all about it," he coaxed.

Rose May went on like the puppet she was, being led by Satan's puppet master.

The next day came, and Reverend Jones took Rose May home. Rose was sitting on the couch anxiously awaiting their arrival. When they entered the door, Rose jumped up and hugged her daughter so tight she didn't want to let her go.

"Oh, baby, I'm so glad to see you! It's all right, everybody makes mistakes. I just thank the Lord you are home and Reverend Jones is here to help you," Rose said.

Rose May shot the good reverend a shameful glance as she looked over her mother's shoulder still in her embrace.

"That's right, Sister Rose, I told her God is a good God, a forgiving God, and He'll keep her."

"Thank you so much, Reverend Jones, for being here with us at this time," Rose praised.

"Oh, it's my duty, Sister Rose. I'm a servant to God's people."

Rose May was in love with him, but in her mind, she was thinking, *What a smooth-talking lying bastard!* He had her mother completely snowed!

"Well, Sister Rose, I'd better be going. I've got some errands to run and some people to serve. God's work is never done. Sister, you keep your head up. God has you in His hands, and you know you're always, always in my prayers," he said, giving Rose May a pastorly pat on the shoulder.

"How much longer will you be in town, Reverend?" Rose asked.

"Oh, I'm catching a late flight out tomorrow," he said nervously.

Rose May's head turned toward him so fast her neck popped. He didn't mention anything to her about leaving tomorrow. She thought he would be here at least another week. Why hadn't he mentioned it to her? They hadn't made any plans.

"Well, Reverend, at least let me cook you a meal tonight before you leave," Rose offered.

"That sounds nice, Sister Rose, but I don't want you to go to any trouble for me," he said grinning and showing all thirty-two of his pretty white teeth.

"Oh, it's my pleasure especially after all you've done to help my baby girl. How's seven sound?"

"Sounds great! I'll see you then," he said, hugging Rose, then giving Rose May a quick hug, and he was out the door.

"Rose May, come over here and sit down, I want to talk to you," Rose asked very patiently.

"Please, Ma, I'm really tired, I don't feel like talking."

"Well, you better bring your tired ass over here and listen!"

Rose May knew when her mother threw in a curse word, she was dead serious. So she went over and sat on the couch beside her.

Rose took her daughter's hand, looked lovingly at her, and began, "Baby, I don't exactly know what's going on inside you, but God knows, and He can fix anything. You're such a beautiful girl, and I love you. Don't be so hard on yourself and stop thinking you're such a bad person. I know God wouldn't let anything that bad come out of me."

Rose May's eyes began to well up with tears because she knew how much her mother loved her, and she would do anything to help her. The demon of guilt engulfed her as she sat there unable to look in her mother's beautiful loving eyes. She so wanted to confess what was going on with her and the good Reverend Jones, but she just couldn't! She knew it would be like putting a knife in her mother's gut. Rose May just sat there looking and feeling foolish.

All she could say was, "Sorry, I'm sorry, Momma."

Rose kissed her gently on the forehead, and said, "Go get you some rest. I know you're tired. I'll start getting some supper ready when Reverend Jones gets here."

Rose May went to her room and sat there with all of her demons ministering to her. She thought, *Reverend Jones, you mean reverend full of shit!* She felt like such a fool. Deep down inside, she knew that nigga was full of game, but she still held on to his empty promises. She felt worthless, and even worse, when she glanced in the mirror, there was that hideous monster again! She looked like a blimp! How could anybody want her? She was a mess! She immediately went to the bathroom to throw up.

"Rose May, you sick?" Rose hollered down the hall.

She didn't mean to do it so loud. "No, Ma, I'm fine."

Rose May returned to her room still feeling the same even after throwing up. As she lay on her bed, she fell asleep with all of her demons sleeping right along beside her.

21

"Rose May, Rose May, get up it's six o'clock. Reverend Jones will be here by seven," Rose shouted down the hall.

Rose May didn't realize she had been asleep that long. She got up, showered, and began the task of getting ready. The reason she felt like it was a task is because she really didn't feel like entertaining the good reverend tonight. She didn't know why she was feeling that way.

As she was getting herself together, she was pondering over the last couple of weeks she'd spent with him, thinking about the things they had talked about, the great sex they had had, the nice gifts he had bought her, and the promises he had made to her. She just couldn't help but wonder why he hadn't told her he was leaving in the morning.

Rose May could smell the aroma of the fried chicken her momma was famous for floating down the hallway. She was very hungry she'd just realized she hadn't really eaten in a couple of days.

"Rose May, come on and eat." Rose hollered.

"Okay, Ma, I'm coming."

As Rose May was setting the table, Rose noticed the solemn look on her daughter's face.

"What's wrong, baby? You used to be so happy when Reverend Jones was coming over. Y'all counseling sessions been goin' okay?"

"Yeah, Ma, I'm just a little tired, that's all."

Well seven o'clock came, no Reverend Jones. And he was always early or on time. Seven-thirty came, no Reverend Jones. Eight-thirty came, Nine-thirty came now, by then, Rose May realized he wasn't coming.

"That isn't like Reverend Jones," Rose said. "Something must have come up. Looks like he would have called though."

Rose May didn't say a word; she just kissed her mother on the cheek and said good night.

"Good night, baby. If Reverend Jones call, I'll let you know."

Rose May retreated to her room and sat on her bed as if in a daze. She just wouldn't let the thought enter her mind that he had left without saying a word. Didn't he say he loved her and would take care of her? Wasn't she his baby doll? Rose May felt like such a jackass. She then thought about Aunt Minnie. She was right! Niggas ain't good but for one thing—money! Just then, an emotion of rage engulfed her.

"That no-good, rotten, lying black ass son of a bitch. If I ever see that nigga again, I'll slit his throat!"

"Who you back there cursing at?"

Rose May hadn't even realized she was talkin' out loud. "Nobody, Ma!"

"You talking to somebody you haven't lost your mind have you?"

"No, Ma. I'm going to bed."

Rose May went to bed, but she didn't sleep at all. All she could think about was how she had allowed herself to be played by that smooth-talking, good-looking bastard. She was hurt truly, truly hurt. She made a vow that night as she cried herself to sleep, she wasn't going to ever let no man say one damn word about love. And she wasn't ever going to allow herself to be in love. What the hell is love anyway?

22

The next day was hard for Rose May.

"I didn't hear a word from Reverend Jones last night," her mother yelled down the hall as she got ready for work. "What you got planned for the day, Rose May?" Rose asked inquisitively.

"Nothin', Ma," Rose May answered dryly.

"Well I left some money on the table. I need you to go out and run a few errands for me. Pay a few bills I'm working a double today. I probably won't get home 'till midnight. You can eat what I fixed for dinner last night and straighten up while I'm gone. There's about two hundred to take care of everything. You hear me?"

"Yeah, Ma, I hear you. I'll get it done."

"Okay, baby, I'm gone. I'll see you when I get home. Bye."

"Bye, Ma."

Rose May immediately popped out of bed after she heard he door slam. She didn't even brush her teeth. As a matter of fact, she still had her pajama pants on. She grabbed up the money off the table and went to cop a slab.

Rose May was pissed off and hurt. She decided she would only take a hundred dollars with her, and when she finished smoking that up, she'd come home. Didn't work like that. After about two hours, she was back for the other hundred. She changed clothes and got fly because she knew when that last hundred was gone, she was going to have to make some money. She wasn't even thinking about telling her mom about the bill money. She'd worry about that later. Right now, she was on a mission.

Rose got home that morning about 2:00 a.m. She was absolutely exhausted. The house was dark. She flipped on the light in the kitchen, and it was still in the same shape she had left it in. Rose thought to herself. *That girl didn't do anything I told her to do!* Rose continued to the bathroom to shower and get ready to lie down. She just assumed Rose May was in her room asleep. She decided to look in on her after she finished showering and dressed for bed. After Rose got dressed, she headed down the hall, cracked the door to Rose May's room, and immediately her heart sank. She wasn't there. Rose turned on the light, went in, sat on the bed, and let out a loud gut-wrenching scream. She knew she wouldn't be seeing her baby girl anytime soon.

Rose May had been gone for a week now. Spring break was over, and school had started, but she didn't care. All Rose May was thinking about was getting beamed up. She was so hurt on the inside she didn't care about anything or anyone else. Rose May went from crack house to crack house, dope man to dope man. She had been smoking crack for seven days straight—no food, no sleep, no bath, no sense.

While out on her mission, she ran up on one of the finest, biggest dope dealers in town. His name was Reno. When Reno stepped in the house that was full of smoke, he spotted Rose May.

"What's a fine thing like you doing beamin' up?"

Even though Rose May had been out for seven days straight with no sleep, she was still beautiful. Not your average-looking smoker. Rose May was on her last dub, and when she saw Reno, she saw dollar signs and rocks. It was time for her to spit game and work her magic as she usually did. When Rose May was on a mission, she didn't stop 'till she got what she wanted, and I mean, all she wanted.

Reno walked over to Rose May, looked at her and said, "Come on, I'm getting you outa here. You goin' wit' me. Fine as you is, you can smoke all you want." That's all Rose May wanted to hear.

"What's yo name?" Reno said as he looked Rose May up and down greedily.

"Rose May."

" What you doin' in there wit them beamers?"

"I smoke," said Rose May.

"You too damn fine to smoke that shit!"

"I ain't fine. I'm a mess," said Rose May.

"Well I'm gon' take you somewhere where you can chill and be comfortable. It's not what you do. It's how you do it. You feel me?"

"Yeah," said Rose May. She didn't care long as she could smoke.

Reno was a good-looking man. He was tall, light-skinned with green eyes and curly, sandy hair. Rose May didn't care if he looked like the boogeyman.

"Where we goin'?" said Rose May.

"I got a few spots we can chill at." How long you been out here?"

"About seven days." said Rose May nonchalantly.

"That's a damn shame fine as you is," said Reno. "I'm gon' take you to get some clothes and things you need to get yourself together. Then you can chill wit me long as you want. How's that sound?"

"Sounds great," said Rose May.

Rose May knew she had hit that jackpot. She was thinking to herself it's on now. But little did she know she was digging her hole to hell deeper and deeper.

Rose was at home in pure torment. She had neither seen nor neard from Rose May in two weeks now. Work, home, worry, cry. Work, home, worry, cry: she had been going through the last week as if she was in some kind of dreamworld. This particular day, she figured out she'd left out one important thing to her monotonous circle—prayer. She hadn't prayed. She hadn't gone to church. She had been so consumed with worry and fear that she had forgotten about God. She immediately fell on her knees and began to cry out to her Heavenly Father, "Lord God in heaven, you know, you see everything. Lord, save my child ."

"Mercy, Lord, mercy. Please have mercy on us." She just lay there in the middle of the floor on her face crying, crying so hard her belly hurt.

The phone rang. Rose was almost scared to answer it, but she did anyway.

"Hello," she said sorrowfully.

"Hey, sister Rose, it's Bessie. We ain't seen nor heard from you. Is everything okay?"

Rose tried to answer without crying, but the tears flooded the phone receiver.

"What is it, child? Somebody dead or something?" Bessie asked worriedly.

"No, Bessie, it's Rose May. I haven't seen or heard from her in two weeks!

"It's going to be alright. Can I come over and talk to you? I think there are some things you need to know." Bessie asked.

"Okay," Rose said as she hung up the phone.

Bessie was knocking on the the door in what seemed like two seconds later.

"Rose!" Bessie said as Rose answered the door and let her in. "You look a mess!"

"I know, Bessie. I can't help it. I'm worried to death.

"Rose May done went back out there and got on that stuff again, ain't she?"

"Yes, Lord, and I don't know where she is."

"I don't know how to begin to tell you this, Rose."

"What? What? What you know, Bessie?"

"Well," Bessie began, "when that old slick talking up the road road preacher Reverend Jones was here. Him and Rose May was layin up at the Shady Oak Motel about every night."

Rose's eyes widened in disbelief. "Bessie, now you lyin'!"

"I hope God may kill me, Rose. You know my cousin Linda Mae works out there. She say she seen them every night."

Rose felt like she would explode with anger. "That no-good-for-nothing, lying, black-ass nigga! I trusted him with my baby girl. I should have known something wasn't right. Rose May started acting real funny at the end now that I think about it."

"It gets worse," Bessie said. "Well they say they done seen Rose May riding around with that dope-dealing pimp Reno."

"Lord, have mercy!" cried Rose. "Bessie, what I'm going do? What I'm going do?"

"Child, all you can do is put it in the hand of the Lord. Come on and go to church tonight. We'll all pray about it. You know the Lord can do anything."

"I reckon that's all I can do, Bessie, that's all I can do."

23

While Rose was in church praying, Rose May was out with Reno partying it up. Or so she thought. Reno had gone out and bought her some new clothes, shoes, underwear, toiletries, and anything else she needed. He'd set Rose May up at the Sky Light Inn where she could smoke and drink all she wanted.

Rose May thought she had it going on! She was with one of the finest, biggest dope men in town, and she wasn't wanting for anything. Reno gave her all the dope she wanted and even supplied the paraphernalia. Not to mention, he kept her stocked with cigarettes, liquor, and beer. He kept Rose May so high she didn't even realize she was being set up to be his number 1 whore. The one thing Reno left out on his resume was that he was also the biggest pimp in town. He had already had his eye on Rose May. He'd seen her on the block a few times. He knew she was fine, and he knew she was a gold mine. He'd finally gotten his clutches in her. He would've pounced sooner if he'd know she was strung out in the base like that.

Man, could this chick smoke, he thought to himself as he watched her drop rock after rock on her stem. She even had about three stems going at one time.

"Hey, Rosie, baby, you better slow down. We got plenty of time, plenty of time."

Rose May was so high she was delirious. She hadn't had any sleep. She didn't want to think about what a mess her life was. She's been made to look like a pure fool, thinking she was in love. She'd missed registration for school. She'd spent her mother's bill money, hadn't talked to her mother in almost three weeks, and she knew her mother was worried to death. And to top it all off, she'd missed her period! *What else could possibly happen other than death?* she thought.

Rose May was soon getting ready to find out. Reno was getting ready to change up. He figured this bitch was smoking too damn much. She was putting him in the red. Instead of an addition, she was becoming a subtraction. He switched to business mode.

"Rosie! Rosie!"

Rose May was so consumed with pushing her stem she didn't even hear him call her.

Reno got up and smacked the stem out of her hand.

"Bitch, you think you playin' me? I ain't no punk-ass nigger. I done set you up an' kept you straight, and you ain't even tried to give me no play! This shit finna stop right now. Get yo ass up. Get in that shower and on this bed. It's time for me to check my inventory!"

Rose May sobered up for a moment.

"What you talking about, Reno? You ain't say nothing about trickin'."

"You think I put out all this bread for nothing? Hell, you done smoked up in the thousands. You owe me, bitch, and I'm gon' get me. Now let's get busy!"

Rose May had fallen in a big trap. She knew Reno owned her now, and there was nothing she could do. She got up and did as she was told. When Rose May got out of the shower, Reno was on the bed, waiting.

"Turn around. Let me see what I got. Nice, real nice. I knew I had a moneymaker. Now come on, and I want the works!"

After Reno finished testing his new product, he was very satisfied.

"Girl, you good. If you wasn't so strung out on that base, I'd make you my woman, but I'm a businessman first, and you way in the hole. I'm sure wit what you workin' with we'll be even real soon. Don't look so sad, baby. Your future gon' be real bright now that you wit me. I'm gon' make you a number one ho! Niggas gon' be lined up for you!"

Rose May couldn't say a word. She felt like an old rotten bag of trash.

"You ain't got nothin' to say?"

Rose May looked up and said, "Yeah, I want another hit."

The true pimp came out in Reno when he heard that. He smacked Rose May so hard she saw stars.

"How was that hit, bitch? You gon' get yo ass dressed and get on that block and make some money! Now get busy! Put on that tight leopard-print minidress I bought you yesterday."

Rose May didn't speak. She just did as she was told, went into the bathroom, tried to pretty herself up, and came out.

"Damn, you fine!" Reno said. "Now go get me my money, bitch!"

Rose May was in pure hell. She felt like killing herself. While she was out on the block, the only thing she focused on was her next hit of dope. *Think mission, mission, mission,* that's what she told herself. Rose May was back at the the room within two hours with six hundred! She handed it over to Reno. He counted it and was grinning from ear to ear.

"I knew you was good, but I didn't know you was that damn good! I guess I'll let you take the rest of the night off. Here, here's a little something for you."

He threw Rose May a whole eight ball.

"I'll be back. I gotta go check my other spots. Remember, you mine now. Don't look so sad, baby. Reno gon' take good care of you, real good care."

As he closed the door, Rose May immersed herself in the freshly cooked eight ball and forgot about anything or anyone.

24

Rose had gone to church that night with Bessie and the girls, and afterward they went out to grab a bite to eat. She did have to admit she felt better after singing and praying at church. Bessie had been a comfort to her the past few days. She'd just come to the conclusion that she was powerless over Rose May. She'd turned it totally over to God.

As soon as she was finally getting it together and getting back into the swing of working and going back to church and socializing with her church friends, up jumped the devil. This was the fourth week she had not seen or heard from Rose May. She had gotten home from work around nine that night; and she opened the door, looked down the hall, and saw a light in Rose May's room.

Rose dropped everything, ran down the hall, burst through the door, and there she was!

"Rose May! Rose May! My baby, my baby! God answered my prayers. Baby, I'm so happy to see ya. Don't worry about nothing. Mama's here!"

Rose May just sat there on the bed, looking as if she'd been in a wrestling match. Her face was gaunt. Her hair was tousled. She lost about twenty pounds; and she smelled like a mixture of smoke, alcohol, and sweat. Rose didn't care. She hugged her so tight she almost crushed Rose May's fragile bones.

"Oh, Momma, I'm in a pickle. I don't know what to do. I'm in trouble," Rose May said.

"What is it, baby? Just tell me. We can work it out. I'm just glad you alive. God spared ya. He showed us mercy. Don't lie to me."

Rose May looked down at the floor. She was ashamed at the way she was looking and smelling in front of her mother. Nevertheless, she began at the beginning and told Rose the whole horrendous story.

Rose just sat there after she finished. With the most loving and understanding look on her face, she said, "Baby, you living. We can work it out with the help of the Lord."

The only part Rose May left out was the part about missing her period and that Reno may be looking for her. She'd figured that was just a little too much for her mother to handle in one night.

"Ma, I'm sorry. I'm really sorry. I love you, Ma, and I'm sorry," Rose May said pitifully.

"You just go get yourself cleaned up, and I'm going to go put on a good pot of beans, fry some chicken, and get some of that weight back on you. We'll worry about the rest later."

As Rose May got up and went to shower, Rose looked upward and said, "Thank you, Lord. Thank you!"

Rose took the next few days off work to take care of Rose May. She had a sinking feeling in her gut that Rose May hadn't told her everything. The next morning, the phone rang. It was Bessie.

"Rose May made it in, Bessie."

"Oh, Rose, praise the Lord!" Bessie said. "I told you the Lord wasn't going fail you. How she doing?" Bessie asked.

"She's doing as well as can be expected, Bessie. We just gotta keep her lifted up to the Lord."

"You know we gon' be prayin' for you, Rose. Let me know if there is anything I can do for you."

"Okay, Bessie. Bye, thank you."

Rose peeped in on Rose May, who was sleeping so hard she didn't think an earthquake could've waked her. Rose May just ate and slept for about two days. On the third day she was home, Rose May was feeling a lot better, but she still had those demons ministering to her. She needed to tell her mother the rest of her predicament. Rose May got up, went into her mother's room, and sat at the bottom of her bed.

"Momma, I need to tell you something."

O Lord, said Rose to herself. "What is it, baby?"

"Momma, when I was out there, I told you I got hooked up with that pimp Reno. He might be looking for me."

Rose sat straight up in the bed and got mad all over again.

"I wish that no-good-for-nothin', dope-pushing bastard would come around here looking for somebody! He won't have to worry about looking for nobody else. I ain't scared of them street niggas! I'll put a bullet in his ass!" Rose screamed uncontrollably.

"What he gon' be looking for you for? You don't owe him nothin', do you?" Rose inquired.

"No, Momma. But he think I belong to him," Rose May said sorrowfully.

"You ain't nobody's property but God's and mine! Don't you worry about that. The day he comes around here looking for somebody will be the day he'll be goin' to hell!"

Rose May knew her momma didn't play and would stand up to anybody, especially when it came to her.

"Well, Momma, there's one more thing." Rose May paused. "I think I'm pregnant." Rose May jumped off the bed because she expected a smack.

Rose sat there in silence for a minute.

"Whose is it?"

"Reverend Jones, Ma."

Rose got mad all over again.

"That lying black son of a bitch. If I could get my hands on him, I'd kill him dead! I knew it, I knew it! Rose May, how could you be so stupid? You know that man didn't love you. I told you about them smooth-talking, up the road niggas. I suppose he told you he was gon' come back to get you, didn't he? I know he did! And he was supposed to be a man of God. That nigga gon' bust hell wide open! Well, it's partly my fault too. I should have known you was too good looking to be spending all that time with that nigga! I'll take the blame for this one. You should have used something, Rose May!"

"Ma, he told me he loved me!"

"That nigga didn't love you. He loved what you was givin' him every night. I knew all about it. Bessie and all them women knew. I'm so ashamed I don't know what to do! Well, you done did it and you might as well sit yo ass down somewhere because you gon' to have this baby, and you gonna take care of it. An' I ain't putting up with no more of yo shit, girl, you hear me?"

"Yes, Mam," Rose May said shamefully.

"Well, go on get out my face, Rose May. I'm mad right now. I gotta go to bed."

Rose May got up sorrowfully, went down the hall to her room, and closed the door.

25

The next few months were hard for Rose May. She knew she was pregnant, but she still wanted to get high. She felt like a pure idiot.

Rose was watching Rose May like a hawk.

"Rose May, you got a life inside you that didn't ask to be here, and that's the most important thing. It ain't all about you no more."

Rose May actually started to feel a little better after she got over the morning sickness. Her mother was with her every step of the way. Rose went to every doctor's appointment with her, made sure she took her vitamins, and fed her good. After Rose got over her madness, she actually began to get excited about the birth of her first grandchild. Rose made Rose May go to church, Bible study, and every other church function going on.

Rose May knew not to complain because she had put her mother through so much in the past few months. She felt like such a failure. Her mother tried to persuade her to go back to school, but Rose May just didn't have the energy or the will. She was just ready for this baby thing, as she called it, to be over. She knew she wasn't finished getting high, but she knew she had to have a healthy baby. Her mother would kill her! That, she knew for a fact.

Rose May wasn't ready for motherhood. She just wasn't. It didn't matter it was here, and she might as well get ready. The months passed by slowly and miserably. Rose May just sat around the house, went to church, and watched TV. Rose was actually happy. Rose May was there with her, and she was going to be a grandma. Even though everybody was talking, Rose still held her head up high. She was a proud woman. After all, she had her precious Rose May by her side.

26

Christmas was approaching, and Rose May was about to pop! The baby was due any day now. Rose May had done very good during her pregnancy as far as staying away from the dope. Besides, Rose was watching her like a hawk. Rose had accumulated so much leave time at her job she was able to stay with her during most of her pregnancy. Rose May had physically stayed away from the dope, but mentally she was still there and couldn't wait, as she so often put it, "to drop this load." Rose knew Rose May wasn't through with the drugs, but she thought that maybe, just maybe, motherhood would change her. After all, it had changed Rose.

Rose May had managed during the pregnancy to slip in a drink here or there, or puff on a joint or two, after which she was consumed with guilt. She just couldn't help it! She knew that if her baby came into the world with anything wrong with it, her mother would absolutely kill her. So she tried her best to stay straight.

Rose was bustling around on this particular day full of joy and song. She didn't care about Rose May's sour attitude anymore. She was going to be a grandma, and she was proud of it!

"Rose May! Get off yo sorry ass and help wrap some of these gifts. You might as well get happy because that baby is gonna be here any time."

"Hey, Momma, I don't see what the big deal is about Christmas. And I don't see why you done gone out and bought all this stuff. We don't even know what the baby is. Boy or girl!"

"I'm big as a house. Ain't no man ever gonna want nothing to do with me!" said Rose May.

"You've had enough men to last a lifetime!" Rose snapped.

Rose May rolled her eyes. Just as she rolled them back the other way, she felt a sharp pain hit and water trickle down her leg.

"Ma, Ma! My water done broke!"

Rose ran over to her excitedly, rubbing Rose May's belly, saying, "It's time, it's time! Let me call Bessie. She gon' take us to the emergency room!"

Rose May cried. "It hurts! It hurts!"

Rose was scurrying around the apartment, looking from place to place to find any number she could find. Just then, there was a knock at the door. Rose rushed to the door, peeped out the window. It was Bessie.

"Lord, Bessie come on in here. This girl finna' have this baby. We gotta go to the emergency room!

"I knew it, I knew it. The Holy Ghost told me to come over here! Let's go!"

Rose and Bessie were on each side of Rose May, with Rose May moaning with each step.

"Oooh, Momma. Oooh, Momma. It hurts so bad," Rose May cried.

"Oh, hell! Shut up. It wasn't hurting that bad when you was getting it! Every time I think about you and that no-good-for-nuthin', slick-talking, supposed-to-be preacher, I get mad all over!" Rose said as she popped Rose May upside the head.

"Ow, Ma," said Rose May. She didn't know whether she was saying *ow* from the pop upside her head or from the pain in her belly.

"Rose, now don't go getting all pissed off all over again. It's done happened and it's done. We gon' have us a baby in no time! Wonder what color it's gon' be?" said Bessie.

"Black! Black, like its old black-ass daddy!" said Rose still mad at Reverend Jones as well as Rose May.

"Mama, please, please don't start now!" said Rose May.

Rose calmed down and got excited about being a grandmother again.

"I'm sorry, baby. You all right? Just breathe easy," said Rose as they got in the car and pulled off.

The next time they came home, their lives would have a new addition.

27

"Oh, he so cute! That's a fine boy you got there, Rose," said Bessie as she stood over Rose May.

"Yes, he is! With his cute little black self. That's the prettiest black baby I've ever seen," said Rose.

Rose May was holding her baby, thinking, *They act like I ain't even here. Who do they think went through all the pain and agony?* Rose May did have to admit he was gorgeous, so handsome. He looked just like his daddy! She definitely didn't need any DNA test to tell her that!

"What you call him, Rose May?" said Bessie.

Before Rose May could open her mouth, Rose shouted from the kitchen, "Lija! We gon' call him Lija like Elijah in the Bible." Rose ran from the kitchen and scooped up little Elijah Jones Carlisle. Rose May rolled her eyes at her mother. She acted as though she was invisible.

"Wasn't Jones his daddy's name?" said Bessie.

"Yeah," said Rose. "But he's the very spit of him. I had to put his name in here somewhere!"

Rose acted like Elijah was her baby instead of Rose May's.

Rose May felt miserable. Not only was she fat; she was invisible. Everybody who came by just came by to see the baby and to see how much he looked like that preacher from New York. Rose May racked up on gifts even though they were just nosey gifts.

"That's right, it's Grandma Rose," Rose said in baby talk as she held Elijah with a crowd of the nosey gift givers around her.

"This Grandma Rose, baby, and ain't nobody gon' never take you away. No, they ain't," Rose said in more of her baby talk.

Rose May stood in the background just looking at her mother you would think Elijah was hers, and she had just given birth. She wanted to go smack her mother the way she had gotten cursed out about that baby and his daddy. Now all she could hear about was Elijah this and Elijah that. Rose acted as if Rose May was incapable of taking care of her own baby. When she tried to feed him, all she heard was don't do it like this, do it like that. She didn't change him right, didn't burp him right, didn't dress him right, and didn't hold him right! Rose May had had it! She just turned the care of Elijah over to Rose who was happy. Rose even took some kind of grandma maternity leave! *The nerve of her*, thought Rose May. All Rose May wanted to do was get her strength and figure back. She'd show her a thing or two!

Elijah was three months old now, and he was a good baby. Rose May had to admit he wasn't a bit of trouble. She loved her son, but it just didn't sound right, or feel right, or something. *I'm somebody's momma*, Rose May thought as she held Elijah. He was so cute. His skin was as smooth as the finest woven silk in India, and his hair was like little black velvet curls all over his head. He had the same dimple on the left side of his cheek just like his daddy. Rose May loved her baby, but she couldn't help but feel a sharp pang of hurt in the middle of her heart when she looked at him. This was her love child. The only time she really had any special moments with Elijah was when Rose wasn't hovering around. Rose May truly loved little Elijah, but she had another lover calling her, and it wouldn't be too long before she would answer.

28

Spring was here, and it was a beautiful day. Rose was in the kitchen, frying a batch of her famous fried chicken, and Rose May was on the porch with Elijah.

Tony pulled up. "Hey, girl, or should I say, hey, momma?" Tony yelled.

"Oh shut up, Tony!" Rose May laughed.

"Girl, it's good to see you! You still fine as ever," Tony said.

"Aw, go on, Tony. You know I ain't looking good," said Rose May coquettishly. After all, she hadn't been close to a man in months, and she had to admit Tony was looking fine.

"That's a petty baby you got, Rose May. Everybody been talking about how cute he is. Can I hold him?" asked Tony.

"Yeah, boy, you know you can!" said Rose May lustfully.

"Whats his whole name?" asked Tony.

"Elijah Jones Carlisle. I call him EJ," said Rose May, scooting closer to Tony.

"You sure do smell good, Tony," said Rose May.

"You do, too, like milk," Tony said jokingly, pinching Rose May on her cheek.

"Go on, boy. Who you go wit now, Tony?" Rose May asked.

"I was seeing Sherry Walker, but it didn't work out," said Tony, looking down at Elijah longingly.

"Oh, I heard that," said Rose May. "She left and went up the road with some man, didn't she?"

"Yeah," said Tony with a frown. "What is it y'all girls love about them-up-the-road niggas?" he asked.

"I don't know, Tony," said Rose May.

"You wanna go to a movie or something sometime?" she asked, trying to change the subject.

"Rose May, you know you too fast for me. You know I always been in love wit you and every time you give me yo ass to kiss."

"Aw, Tony, go on now. You know it ain't like that," said Rose May.

Just then, Rose appeared in the door.

"Hey, Tony, baby. How you doin'?"

"Fine, Miss Rose, fine," Tony said.

"You wanna stay for dinner? I just fried some chicken. I got more than enough," said Rose.

"Yeah, Tony. You know you still greedy," teased Rose May.

"Okay," said Tony. He was still feeling Rose May, and to him she'd always been beautiful—fat or skinny, clean or sober. Rose May was feeling differently about Tony only because that lust demon was ministering to her. Little did Tony know he'd better put on his running shoes because Rose May was getting ready to run him ragged.

29

Tony had started dropping in to visit Rose May on a regular basis and taking her and Elijah out. Rose felt contented. She liked Tony. She always did think he was a nice boy. She knew he genuinely cared about Rose May, and she knew her baby boy, Lija, was safe.

"Rose May!" Rose called. "Date with Tony? You and Tony supposed to be gon' together." Rose pryed.

"No Momma. You know me and Tony been friends since we was little. That don't mean nothing," Rose May said. "You're too nosey Rose."

Rose said, "he always has been a nice boy. He come from good people, and he got some good home trainin'."

Rose May rolled her eyes up in the air and said, "Momma, please! Tony and me just friends. I told you stop trying to marry me off to to the first man that comes around!" Rose May snapped.

"I ain't tryin' to marry you off. It's just that you need to settle down. You got a child now. What you planning on doin' with yourself?" Rose asked inquisitively. "You ain't got

n't move her jaw. All she called do was
as her eyes vibrated.
aid Daniel. "I told you it was some of

May got her composure back and jaw
uld do was shake her head. "Daniel,
o da fire!" Rose May said.
" said Daniel. And it was on!
aniel were from spot to spot that night,
ng, smoking and drinking. Rose May
inside. When she thought about her
cially Elijah, she just had to get high.
rewed up, and screwed up badly, so to
mind, she had to stay high. She had

e, girl. You smoking hard and strong!"

up with Rose May? After all, Rose
h up and she had a lot of emotions

days, and Rose May was still going
n., and she and Daniel were headed
me beer. As Rose May was headed
our forty-ounce Colt 45, she heard
y, "Bitch! Where the hell you been?
s for months, and I catch you ridin'
ot!" Rose May almost jumped out

back in school, and Lija's almost five months old!" Rose said agitatedly.

"Momma, don't start!" Rose May said loudly. "I ain't ready to settle down, and if I was, it wouldn't be with Tony!" Rose May screamed.

"You don't like nice boys," said Rose, getting wound up. "You like them old low-life, no-count, good-for-nothing niggas that can run you like a po' dog!"

Rose May was fuming! She was sick and tired of her mother's mouth always putting her down, making her feel worthless. Rose May knew Tony would be there in thirty minutes, but she couldn't wait. She couldn't stand it in her mother's presence another minute. She needed to drink and she needed to drink now! Rose May picked up Elijah, kissed him, gave him to her mother, and slammed the door.

Rose jumped up with Elijah in tow, opened the door, and yelled to her, "Where you goin'! You know Tony comin'."

"I ain't waiting on him!" Rose May hailed a car passing and jumped in.

Rose stood in the door, looking crazy.

"That foolish-ass girl! I know where she gone. I know!" Rose stated. "It's gon' be all right, baby. Grandma Rose gon' take care of you."

About twenty minutes later, there was a knock on the door. Rose peeped out. It was Tony looking excited and happy. Rose hated to open the door. She slowly opened the door. Tony could tell by the grim look on her pretty face something was wrong. "What is it, Miss Rose?" asked Tony.

"She gone, Tony. She just walked out. Walked out on me an' Lija. She knew you were coming. She just got mad and ran off. I know where she gone," said Rose disappointedly. "She gone to get high. I thought after Lija was born all that was done, but I guess it ain't," Rose said as a tear rolled down her cheek and dripped onto Elijah's forehead.

Tony put his hand on Rose's shoulder and said, "I don't think so, Miss Rose. I'll go look for her. I don't believe she gonna smoke anymore! She told me she was through with that." Tony looked down pitifully at Elijah and kissed him on the head. "I'll be back, and I'll be back with Rose May!"

"Good luck. Tony, I'll pray I'll be right here with my baby." said Rose as Tony turned, jumped in his car, and sped off.

Tony looked in every liquor house and dope hole he knew and could inquire about. No Rose May. Tony felt real bad as he pulled up in front of Rose May's house without her. He had looked for five hours.

Rose heard the car pull up as she had just put Elijah down. She listened, but she had only heard one door open and close. She ran to the door anyway, expectedly. She saw Tony walking slowly up to the door with his head down. She knew. She met Tony at the door, and they looked in each other's eyes sorrowfully because they didn't know how long it would be before they saw Rose May again.

Rose May could
hold up one finger
"Heellll, yeah!"
that thang, um!"

As soon as Rose
unstuck, all she co
boyfriend, take me t
"Okay, girlfriend
Rose May and D
smoking and drinki
was hurting on the
mom, Tony, and esp
She knew she had s
keep all that off her
no choice!

"Slow down, Rosi
said Daniel.

Who could keep
May was playing cat
to suppress.

It had been three
strong. It was 7:00 a.
to the store to get so
out of the store with
a recognizable voice s
I been' lookin' for yo a
around with this fagg

R ose M
hers
May said
"Hey,
you beer
"I b
Daniel?
her stor
"Yo
sweetie
"N
ain't g
May s
"I
stem,
he p
R
head
"

of her skin and dropped all the beer she was carrying. It was Reno, and he looked like he was going to kill both her and Daniel!

"Daniel, or should I say, Danyale," Reno said. "Bitch, you owe me money too! I'm gon' put both y'all on the block. Get in the car! Both of you!" Daniel and Rose May both got in Reno's car, looking like scared puppies.'

After the three of them got to the Star Light Inn, Reno instructed Daniel to go in the bathroom while he talked to Rose May. He gave him something to smoke on while he "talked" to Rose May.

As Daniel closed the bathroom door, he heard Reno smack Rose May so hard she screamed. But he knew better than to say anything, or he would get worse. He just went in the bathroom and smoked to block out the sound of the blows Rose May was taking. When Reno had finished the brutal beatdown, he called Daniel out of the bathroom, who was shaking not only from the dope but from the beating he was about to get.

When Daniel saw Rose May, he gasped. Her beautiful face was swollen and red, and she had marks all around her neck.

"Bring yo punk ass here! And Rosie, get yo ass in that bathroom and don't come out 'till I say so!" Reno screamed to the top of his voice. "Bitch! Yo punk ass got my money?" Reno asked Daniel.

"Well, honey, I was…"—*punch*! Reno punched Daniel in the mouth so hard his tooth fell on the floor. Daniel immediately started screaming.

"Shut yo punk ass up! That's all I'm gon' do to you! You betta get my money or I'm gonna kill you. Rosie, come on out!

Rose May came out of the bathroom all battered and bruised, still crying.

"Rosie, baby, you know I hated to do dat. But you played me. You belong to me… both y'all. Now get out there an' hustle up my bread. Rosie, you stay here wit me. I need to check my inventory. Danyale, you get on the stroll. I wanna see you back here in two hours wit a bankroll. I'll hook you up when you get back."

Daniel looked pitifully at Rose May. As she returned the glance, he left out.

"Why you run out on me, Rosie?" Reno asked.

"Reno, I got pregnant. I had a baby," Rose said shamefully.

"You what?" It ain't mine, is it?"

"No, Reno, it ain't yours," Rose May said, nursing her wounds.

"Oh, that's good! You still got it goin' on. Now get in that shower an' come on over here an' let me see what I'm workin wit."

Rose May did as she was told, but she was worried. She knew Reno wasn't going to use protection with her, and her womb was wide open. She was even scared to ask him for fear of another beating.

After her initiation was over, Rose May felt like a train had hit her. Her whole body was sore. As she lay there, she began to cry.

"Don't start that shit. I'm gon' give you sumpthin' to smoke, an' I aint even gon' put you on the block for two days. You gon' lay up wit' me for a while." Rose May wasn't crying because she wasn't smoking. She was crying because she missed her baby, and she had gotten her life in such a mess in such a short amount of time.

Reno reached in his pocket and threw her a whole eight ball. "That's goin' on yo tab. You want it?"

Rose May shook her head yes and began her vicious cycle of smoking.

"I'm goin' out to get some beer, liquor, and cigarettes. Don't let nobody in but yo sissy ass friend Danyale.

Rose May was so into her stem he had to go push her. "You hear me, bitch?" Rose May shook her head and continued to smoke.

"Get yo ass up an' lock da door!"

"Okay," said Rose May, happy he was leaving.

31

A month had gone by, and Rose or Tony had not heard a thing from Rose May.

Tony was checking in with Rose daily because he really cared for her and Rose May, and he had become quite attached to little Elijah. Tony would even babysit for Rose on occasion while she went on a few errands. Rose was blessed in that she was now on a private duty sitting job where she could take little Elijah with her. He was the light of her life. Elijah kept her mind off Rose May even though her heart ached with grief because of the life her daughter chose to live. Rose had heard through the grapevine, and boy, did Rose May keep the grapevine busy that she had hooked back up with Reno the pimp.

What could she be thinking? Rose thought to herself as she rocked Elijah to sleep.

"How could she leave this precious thing?" Rose said out loud while in thought, *It's all right, Lija. Grandma Rose is here and I love you wit' your cute little self. Maybe you'll be more than your momma is wit' her crazy...*

Just then, there was a knock at the door. Rose looked out. It was the police! Rose's heart began to pound ferociously.

"Oh, Lord," Rose said as she slowly opened the door while cringing in fear and peeping around it curiously.

"Good evening, mam," the officer said.

"Evening," said Rose very timidly.

"Does Rose May Carlisle live here?" the officer asked.

"Yes, sir. She sure does what's wrong?" Rose asked, her voice trembling.

"We need you to come to the morgue to identify a body. A purse was found alongside the body with this address in it," said the officer.

Rose stood there, as if her spirit had left her body, and she was looking down.

"Mam! Mam!" The officer had to shake her.

"Oh, give me a few minutes to get the baby together." Rose heard the words but, they sounded jumbled and foreign. Had she lost her mind? Was she dreaming? Why wouldn't her legs move? "Help me, Jesus. Help me, Lord. Help me, Jesus. Help me, Lord," Rose mumbled. She couldn't move.

"Mam, do you need to call someone?" the officer said.

"Call someone," Rose repeated.

Just then, Tony drove up and sped up to the door. "What is it, Miss Rose? Whats wrong?" asked Tony.

Rose couldn't say a word. Her eyes were glassy.

"Officer, what is it?" Tony asked. "I'm a friend of the family."

The officer explained the situation to Tony. Tony's heart sank. "Come on, Miss Rose. Where's Lija? Come on, you can do this. I'm here wit' you."

Rose was an emotional wreck. She was moving as if in a daze. Tony grabbed Elijah's diaper bag and the baby and led Rose out to his car. After putting in the car seat and strapping the baby in, he helped Rose in the car. They rode in complete silence all the way downtown. Rose just stared forward, not moving an inch in the car. She was frozen with fear. What if it was Rose May? How could she see her only baby she would ever have dead?

"Miss Rose! Miss Rose! Miss Rose!" Tony had to call her three times. "We're here!" he said emphatically. Tony got out, got the baby, and had to practically pry Rose out of the front seat.

Rose walked slowly up to the automatic doors with Tony guiding her to the morgue.

"Miss Rose! Miss Rose!" Tony almost shouted.

To Rose it sounded as if she was in a tunnel. She could hear herself breathing and hear her heart pounding as she and Tony approached the desk to inquire. She could see the woman's lips moving and her finger point, but all she could hear were her deep breaths and heartbeat. Tony led the way with Elijah in tow. Rose looked up and saw the word *morgue* on the wall. They both sat on the bench and waited. Sweat was beading down on Rose's forehead.

A man in a white jacket came out and called for Rose to come through the steel doors. She didn't even realize she was clutching the bench. Tony gave her a quick nudge. "You need me to go in with you?" Tony asked. Rose shook her head no and proceeded through the doors. Tony sat there for what seemed like two seconds. Rose burst back out of the door, cursing,

"Tony! Bring that baby and come on. That damn crazy ass Rose May gonna kill me if I don't kill her first! Then she'll really be down here on a slab. That idiot. I'm gonna kill her, Tony! If I could get my hands on that cow," Rose continued, walking fast, leaving Tony behind he had to practically run to keep up.

"So it wasn't her?" Tony asked, smiling.

"No, it wasn't. But it's gonna be if I find her! Somebody po' dead child laying in there wit old stupid Rose May's pocketbook!"

32

"Girl, you my number one!" said Reno, smiling as he counted the money Rose May had given him."

"I should be you work me like a dog," said Rose May, sitting down, taking off her shoes, getting her apparatus ready for a megablast.

"Hey, now don't smoke too much of that shit. Your shift ain't over yet, an' you know you get stuck !" said Reno, frowning.

Rose May continued cutting up her dope, as if she hadn't heard a thing. *Bam!* The next thing Rose May knew she was getting off the floor. "Bitch, don't act like you can't hear me. Now get yo trifling ass back on the block. You ain't smoking a damn thang 'till my paper straight!"

Rose May, was sick, she was really jonesing right now. "Damn, Reno, can't I jes' get one hit before I go. Please!" said Rose May, looking up pitifully.

"Hell, no," Reno said as he delivered a swift kick to her side. " Now get to stepping!"

Rose May got up, limping toward the door. She knew she wouldn't have any peace until she got Reno's money, so she went back out on the stroll.

"That no good son of a bitch," Rose May mumbled as she walked the street. "I'm sick of this damn shit! It's my damn money!" she continued. "How did I get hooked up with this fool anyhow!" Just as she finished her sentence, Daniel walked up. Well, he was Danyale tonight.

"Baby, girl, what happened to you? You look a hot damn mess!" said Danyale.

"That no good-fo'-nuthin' bitch-ass Reno won't give me no more dope 'till I hustle up some more bread!" said Rose May.

"Girlfriend, Reno be trippin'. I just paid my tab in full. Come go wit' me. I know a spot we can chill at," said Danyale while pulling Rose May by the arm.

"I gotta get this fool his money girl!" said Rose May emphatically.

"You'll get it. The night still young, girl. Come on."

It didn't take much to persuade Rose May because she was jonesing for a hit, but she knew Reno would be on patrol. She decided to go anyway and worry about Reno later. In the end, she will have wished she'd worried about Reno first.

33

Rose was at home with little Elijah going on with her daily business. She had resigned herself to just go on and turn Rose May over to God once again.

Elijah was getting big. He was almost seven months old. *He was such a good baby*, Rose sat there, thinking to herself as she shelled a bowl of peas. Little Elijah was on the floor, sitting in front of her, playing with one of the shells from the peas. He had no idea what degradation his mother was in out there in the street.

"Poor motherless child," Rose said aloud.

Just as Rose had finished shelling her peas, there was a knock at the door. It was Bessie.

"Hey, Rose, how you doing?" said Bessie as she came in reaching down to pick up Elijah.

"I'm doing as well as can be expected, Bessie. Just living my life, trusting in the Good Master," said Rose as she put her peas on the stove.

"This boy sure is getting big. He's a fine baby. Yes he is. It sure is a shame his momma ain't around to see him," said Bessie as she played with Elijah.

"I know," said Rose sorrowfully. "It jus' ain't nothing I can do, Bessie! I done cried, I done loss sleep, I done prayed, I done done everything I know to do!" said Rose, throwing her hands in the air. "I gotta be here for my baby, Bessie. That boy needs me. His momma running around here half crazy, I don't know if she's after dope or a man. It's a damn shame. Rose May could have been something!" said Rose as she shook her head.

"Well," said Bessie, "I know you gave all you can give. Lord knows you did. Just trust the Lord. He'll see you through." Bessie was rocking little Elijah to sleep. "Turn on the stories, child. They gon' be good today. You know Helen caught James wit that other woman?" said Bessie excitedly as Rose reached for the remote.

As Rose flipped through the channels, she stopped at the news. She saw the news reporter's lips moving, but she couldn't believe what she was hearing. It was Rose May! She had been badly beaten and was at City General. They flashed a picture of the beater being led away in cuffs by the police. "Bessie! Watch Lija, and give me yo keys! I gotta go get my baby!"

Rose flew out the door, jumped in the car, and sped off to City General. Rose was speeding feverishly during which she began to pray aloud, "Lord Almighty God in heaven, please, please let her live! Please, God. You hear me? This yo good and faithful servant, Rose! Please, Lord, have mercy!" Rose pulled up at a screeching halt in front of the hospital. She jumped out so fast she left the car door open.

"Mam, mam!" shouted the security guard.

Rose kept running until she got to the information desk. "Rose May Carlisle! Rose May Carlisle! Where she at!" Rose asked the receptionist breathlessly.

The woman pointed her in the direction of the elevators. Rose couldn't get to the Up button fast enough! "Damn it," Rose said loudly as she dashed for the stairwell. Rose sprinted up the three flights of stairs like a marathon runner. Out of breath, she reached the nurse's station. Her face was flushed, and her heart was beating fast. "Rose May Carlise! Rose May Carlise! I'm her momma!" she breathlessly told the nurse behind the counter.

"Calm down, mam," the nurse said soothingly. "I'll take you to her room. She's going to be fine. She's in room 326."

"326! 326! Where! Where!" Rose said almost in hysterics.

The nurse came around the desk and took Rose's arm with comforting authority and led her to the room. When Rose reached the room, she froze at the door, afraid of what she was about to see.

"It's okay, mam. She's sleeping. I gave her a mild sedative, and the doctor will be in to speak with you shortly," said the nurse as she gently stroked Rose back and turned to walk away. "Just push the nurse's button if you need anything."

Rose walked slowly over to the bed and gasped at what she saw. Her beautiful, beautiful child! She looked at what that monster had done to her baby's beautiful face! Tears were streaming uncontrollably down her face. Rose May looked dead. Her eyes were swollen shut, her lips were swollen with cuts and bruises on them, her jaw looked disfigured, her arm was in a sling, and there was dried, caked-up blood in her once-beautiful hair.

"Oh my God!" Rose said aloud. "My po' child been beat like a po' dawg and left to die!" Rose said as she stroked Rose May's battered and bruised arm.

Rose May felt and tasted her mother's salty tear fall on her once-beautiful full lips. "Oh, Momma," she lamented.

"Hush, child," Rose whispered. "It's gon' be all right. Momma here. The Good Master ain't done wit you."

Rose May felt like she had been hit by a train! "Let me see my face, Ma," she commanded.

Rose just sat there. She couldn't let Rose May see what that monster Reno had done to her once-beautiful face.

"Let me see it, Ma!" Rose May said emphatically.

Rose reluctantly took the mirror from the end table and held it up to Rose May's twisted face. Rose May screamed out, "Jesus!" And tears began to stream down her black-and-blue swollen cheeks. Rose's heart was so sad. But in her mind, she thought at least the girl had called Jesus's name. Just then the doctor came in. Rose was standing by Rose May's bed, watching the doctor's lips move, and the room began to spin. All Rose heard was *twelve-weeks pregnant*. The next thing Rose remembered was her best friend Bessie's voice. "Rose, Rose, Rose, Rose, you all right? You just had a dizzy spell. Rose May gon' be all right. She done got herself big again, Rose," said Bessie.

Rose felt like crawling in a hole after she kicked the shit out of Rose May. *How could she be so stupid!* Rose thought to herself. She looked over at Rose May who was sleeping so soundly, as if she didn't have a care in the world. *Well*, Rose thought, *I've got to be strong for Rose May, Elijah, and the new little bundle of hell on the way.*

34

It was a hot summer, and Rose May was big, very big. Rose May was sitting on the porch just as Daniel strolled by. "Hey, girl," Daniel said. He was of the male persuasion today.

"Kiss my big fat ass," Rose May said. "You the reason Reno almost killed my ass."

"Ain't nobody tell you to follow me to get yo blast on. You know Reno's crazy 'bout his bread girl," said Daniel, filing his nails.

"Where that fool at anyway?" asked Rose May inquisitively.

"Oh, he still in county. He ain't getting out no time soon, child, an' everybody happy as a punk in boy's town. Girl, Reno is a menace to society!" said Daniel now turning into Daniyale, snapping her fingers in the air. "Anywho, moving on, girlfriend. I got this fire from Bay Bay, girl. It's some straight fiyuh! You wanna blast?"

Rose May sat straight up, and her mouth started to water, and her stomach started to churn. She hadn't got off since her beat down from Reno, and she could use a blast. It sure hadn't been easy living here with her mother, taking care of a one-year-old, and not to mention, carrying her pimp's baby that she didn't even want! What justification! "Hell, yeah!" Rose May exclaimed as she jumped up and led Daniyale in the cluttered apartment she was supposed to be cleaning while Rose and Elijah were gone running errands all day.

"Where Momma Rose at?" asked Danyale before stepping across the threshold. "You know she don't like me, an' she'll beat me down worse than Reno about you if she caught us in here blazin'," Danyale said the whole time, getting his stem fixed up and ready.

"She gon' be out all day. Nigga, hurry up. I'm sick," said Rose May pacing, looking around and peeping out the windows. Rose May was now oblivious as to what she was doing she wasn't even thinking about the innocent life growing inside her. All she was thinking about was feeding the hungry crack demon begging for food. "Hurry, yo punk ass-up, Daniel," said Rose May as she secured the apartment stepping over clothes, pulling open drawers, and looking under cushions for a razor to cut her dope. "Got one!" she hollered.

"I don't need it," yelled Danyale from a cloud of smoke in the front room.

"Gimmie me," said Rose May, shaking her stem in front of Danyale.

All Danyale could do was break off a big dub and place it on the stem, she couldn't talk.

Rose May was shaking uncontrollably as she lit the lighter and put the stem up to her lips, so much so that she dropped her hit. She pounced on the floor after it. When she found it, that's where she stayed. When she lit the twenty-cent piece of dope, it fried like bacon. Rose May's eyes vibrated like a ball in a pinball machine, and she was sure she heard a train. Danyale looked down at her on the floor and said, "Girl, you looked shell as hell! I told you that was some fiyuh! Bay Bay don't play. That shit got you mouth movin' an' eveything. You want some more?" said Danyale as she loaded her stem again. "Rose May, get yo dumbass off that floor. You ain't drop no dope down there! I got plenty more dope in my pocket. Here!" said Danyale, handing Rose May a whole fifty.

The whole visit was getting out of hand these two fools were acting shell. Danyale was stuck in one spot with dope spread all over Momma Rose's table, Rose May was running from room to room peeping out the windows instead of turning the air conditioner on Rose May turned the heat on, and they were both sweating bullets. Rose May and Danyale had both just taken a blast, and Rose May was peeping out the front blind. Rose May was so high she didn't even see Momma Rose and Elijah come up the walkway. Rose opened the door and the crack smoke rushed out and hit her square in the face. "What the hell!"

Rose exclaimed as she dropped her bags along with Elijah who began screaming in the middle of the living room floor. Rose turned to Rose May and slapped her so hard she saw stars. "Rose May, what in the hell is wrong with you? And you!" she exclaimed as she approached Danyale who was now trembling in pure fear. "You sissy bitch. I told you not to ever come around my house. Never no more you ain't nothing but a demon strait from the pit a hell. You get yo trifling dope-smoking sissy ass outa here."

Rose had now turned the coffee table over and dope and ashtrays, and whatnots flew everywhere. Danyale flew out of the front door, leaving a piece of his shirt in Momma Rose's hand. Rose turned to Rose May who was standing in the same spot where her mother had assaulted her. She was looking so stupid.

Elijah was still crying, looking up at his mother pitifully. He was only a baby, but his eyes were filled with so much wisdom.

Rose looked down. "Rose May! Yo water done broke! Lord have mercy. Get yo dumbass to the car!" Rose yelled as she scooped up Elijah and yelled next door for Bessie, her right hand.

35

Rose, Bessie, and Elijah sat in the waiting room while Rose May was in with the doctor. Rose was scared to death. Rose May's baby was coming two months early, not to mention Rose May was high on crack in the delivery room.

Rose hadn't breathed a word or this to Bessie or the people at the hospital. All Rose could do was sit still and pray. Pray that the poor innocent child in Rose May's belly had a chance at life. Rose looked up at the ceiling and began to talk to God, "Lord, you know me. This Rose, the same Rose you done brought through so much stuff. I need you, Lord, I need you Lord. That po' little baby need you, Lord. He ain't did nothing to nobody. An' Rose May, Lord, she need You too, Lord. Save them, Lord. Little Lija, he need You too, Lord…"

Just as Rose was finishing her prayer, she heard, "Rose Carlisle."

Rose looked up with tears in her eyes, expecting the worst.

"Yeah," she said wearily.

"Rose May had a boy," the doctor said slowly. Rose breathed in and held her breath. "But," he said, "the baby is underweight. His lungs aren't fully developed."

Rose breathed out so hard she almost collapsed. Bessie held her up and let out an, "Oh, Lordy Jesus!" as she braced her friend tightly and looked down at little Elijah sympathetically.

Rose looked up at the emotionless doctor and asked, "When can I see them?"

The doctor looked at Rose and said, "You can see your daughter now, but the baby will be in NICU. He will have to be up to five pounds before he can go home and completely able to breathe on his own."

Rose had the most worried look on her brow as she was being led in to see Rose May. Rose May was lying on her side with her back to the door as her mother stepped in. Rose could hear Rose May weeping softly. Rose thought to herself as she approached the bed, *I could grab that negro and strangle her!* But as she stood over her now-grown daughter who had two children of her own, and a full-blown drug addiction, her heart began to melt, and she just wanted to grab Rose May up in her arms and rock her like she used to when she was a little girl.

"Hey, baby girl. How you feeling?" Rose said as she stroked her daughter's beautiful hair.

Rose May turned over quickly with a screwed-up face and tears streaming and screamed to her mother, "How you think I'm feelin', Ma! I feel like shit! I ain't got shit, an' I ain't gon' be shit. I just wanna get the hell outa this damn hospital!"

Rose was in shock she felt the color leave her face. "What about the baby, Rose May? Ain't you gon' ask how he's doing, where he's at, when you can see him?" Rose was almost begging.

Rose May shot her mother the most evil glance Rose had seen, rose up on the bed, and said, "I don't give a damn about that baby! I didn't want it nohow!"

Before Rose knew it, she felt the back of her hand on Rose May's face. "Now you listen to me girl," Rose said, now looking like her strong stern self. "That poor baby ain't ask to be born to your trifling ass or his trifling ass daddy! Now that's a blessing from God and you gon' act like if it kill you! That's your blood Rose May! Are you that damn foolish? Do you know drugs done fried yo brain! Now you get yo shit together because you gon' do the right thing by that baby, or I'm gon' have you laid up in this hospital for real!" Rose said.

With all that being said, Rose May knew what time it was when she looked in her mother's hazel eyes and saw her flared nostrils. "You hear me, girl." Rose almost shouted.

Rose May looked timidly at her mother and said, "Yes, Mam," and sunk back down in the bed.

36

"Put out that damn cigarette!" Rose bellowed." You know I don't like all that smoke around Lija. Ezra will be home soon an his po' little lungs can't take that!" Rose went on.

"Okay, Ma!" Rose May said as she smashed half of her Newport 100 in the ashtray.

Rose May was sitting on her front stoop looking out over the neighborhood. *What a shit hole*, she thought to herself and Ezra! *What kind a baby name is that?* Rose May had been home from the hospital only a week and hadn't thought about going to visit the baby. Rose May left everything to do with the new baby up to her mother. Rose was the one going back and forth every day to the hospital to see the baby. Rose even named the baby. When Rose saw the little shriveled-up pink boy who had big sandy locks all over his head, she thought of the book of Ezra because in all her reading and understanding of the Good Book, the book of Ezra taught God's people to find new life in worship of God and to be obedient to God's word. Rose prayed that this baby would do just that for Rose May.

Rose May was just sitting, just thinking. *How did my life come to this?* she pondered. *I got one baby by a supposed-to-be preacher who I thought I was in love wit. That sorry nigga just disappeared. I ain't never gonna trust no God-people. I got this other baby by my pimp!* She sighed. *What a life!* Rose May thought. As she continued to ponder over her situation, she felt her stomach do a dive. Her mouth began to water and she began to look crazy. She knew too well what these symptoms were. Rose May looked down at her hands and they were sweaty. There was a big lump in her throat. She knew she needed her medicine. Rose May didn't give any thought to her mother, Elijah, or little Ezra, who didn't even know he was in the world.

Rose May went in to her closet snatching clothes out, running through drawers, looking for something to put on. She had been out of commission for a while, but she knew she had to look right to get right.

"Rose May! Rose May!" Rose yelled from down the hall. She was occupied feeding Elijah.

"Yeah, Ma?" Rose May answered as she tried to squeeze her voice out past the big lump in her throat.

"What you doin' in there making all that fuss?" Rose said.

"Getting dressed, Ma!" Rose May said with a frown.

"Oh, that's good because I'm tired of seeing you in that old ugly housedress and those old beat up shoes. Get youself fixed up and go see Ezra. He needs to see his momma. You ain't seen him since he was born." Rose went on and on.

"Okay, Ma," Rose May said, as if in a trance. "I'll do that. Yeah, I'll go see the baby."

Rose May said.

Right then, she knew that was her ticket. She knew if she got out, she could get right. All she had to do was find the right nigga to break bread. Even though Rose May had had two babies and been through so much in her short years, she still looked good. None of her beauty had faded, only her spirit. Her eyes didn't posess the sparkle and glow of life they once did when she was a younger girl. Rose May didn't give a damn right now. The only glow she was thinking about was the glow of her BIC lighter being put up.

Rose May stepped out of her room all showerd up and fixed up. Rose looked up at her and said, "Now that's more like it. You look like new money. Rose May, you look like somebody now. Now go to that hospital and see your baby and let's get on wit life." Rose was beaming glad to see her daughter looking better. Little did Rose know Rose May had her moneymakin' clothes in her big pocketbook.

"Okay, Momma, I'm going. I'll be back later. I'm gon' take the car," Rose May said while bending down to give Elijah one of her few and in-between kisses. He looked at her longingly as the scent of her Chanel perfume trailed after her.

"Rose May, call me when you get there. Let me know how Ezra's doing. I just can't make it today. I'm tired," Rose said lazily.

"Okay, Ma," Rose May said as she slammed the door behind her. Little did Rose know that slam would be a slam in the face to her because Rose May was out.

Rose was feeling good this afternoon. So good in fact she had made some of her famous lemonade and some of that delicious fried chicken she was known for.

"Hey, Grandma Rose, something sure does smell good," said the voice coming through the door.

Rose spun around with Elija on her hip to see who the voice belonged to. It was Tony's.

"Hey, boy, how you doing? You know you looking fine," Rose said to the handsome young man as she beamed happily.

"Grandma Rose, it sure is good to see you. Where's Rose May? I heard she had a boy. Where's the baby?" Tony asked, looking around, more anxious than anything to see Rose May. Tony really loved Rose May. He'd loved her since she was a chubby little girl. Tony just didn't understand why Rose May's life had taken such an ugly turn. She was such a pretty girl.

"Tony. Tony!" said Rose.

"Huh? Yes, mam," Tony said as he was shaken out of his daze.

"Rose May went down to the hospital to see the baby. Po' thang, he ain't but three and a half pounds. He can't come home until he gain some weight and his lungs get fully done," said Rose.

"Oh, that's too bad. What did she name him?" Tony asked.

"I named him," Rose said proudly. "His name's Ezra, and he the cutest little thing. He look like a little white baby. I gotta go see him tomorrow po' little thing. He don't even know he's in the world," said Rose as she shook her head.

"How is Rose May doing wit the other thing, Grandma Rose?" asked Tony timidly.

"Well," Rose said as she let out a sigh. "As well as can be expected, she has a spell every now and again, but I really believe to my soul little Ezra done changed her." Rose said, looking hopeful.

"I hope so," said Tony. "I sure do love Rose May, Grandma Rose, and it'll kill me if anything happen to her." Tony said.

"She'll be fine. She gonna call when she get to the hospital. She ain't been gone long. Now sit down and have something to eat," Rose said as she handed little Elijah to Tony and began dipping the golden fried chicken out of the hot grease.

37

Rose May pulled up to the front of the dope house on two wheels, got out of the car, and slammed the door. Rose May was sick not just physically but mentally. While she was driving past the hospital, her supposed destination, she was trying to convince herself that she would only smoke one rock, two at the most, then she would go see that baby and take her mother's car back.

Yeah right! *Bam! Bam! Bam!* Rose May was knocking hard, and sweat was popping off her head.

"Who the hell is it knocking like the police?" said the high-pitched voice from the other side of the door.

"It's Rose May," Rose May said in a weak, out-of-breath voice.

The door swung open. "Hey, bitch," said Daniyale. "When you drop that load?" he said, grinning from ear to ear while pulling Rose May through the door.

"What the hell you doin' here?" said Rose May, grabbing her stomach that was now flipping violently.

"This is my spot now, girlfriend. I got it goin' on! Big T put me down wit my own trap," said Danni, as he was commonly known. Danni had a thousand questions, but Rose May wasn't trying to hear anything but some dope burning on a stem.

"Nigga, I'm sick! We can catch up later. Gimme something for twenty," said Rose May, almost shaking.

"Child, you know we folks. Yo money ain't no good wit me, least not now right now. Come on, girlfriend, I got you," said Danni, pulling out a big plate of cut-up dope from under the bed.

Danni dropped a twenty-dollar rock in Rose May's hand. Rose May reached for her apparatus, her hands trembling, and she fired the whole twenty up! As Rose May inhaled the intoxicating smoke and held it in, she felt her whole inner being lift out of her body. She felt free like she was floating!

"Yeah, Booboo. That's straight fire!" said Danni, standing up snapping her fingers in the air.

Rose May was high, and she didn't give a damn!

38

Rose, Tony, and Elijah finished eating. And Tony was helping Rose with the dishes. "You sit down, Grandma Rose. I'll get this. I know you tired. That meal was outta sight," Tony exclaimed as he rubbed his belly.

"Thank you, baby," Rose said as she scooped Elijah up, who was still sucking a chicken leg bone. "It's been three hours since that girl left here, and I aint heard nothing," said Rose as she rocked Elijah.

"Don't worry," Tony said convincingly. "Grandma Rose, she all right. I know she went to see her baby," said Tony as he dried and put up the last of the dishes.

Rose sighed and looked down lovingly at Elijah who was just as happy as he could be.

"Tony, to be honest with you, I don't think Rose May want nothing to do wit Ezra. She ain't got no love for that baby. I see it. I see it all in her face, Tony. She don't even have no feeling for little Lijah. I'm all the momma he knows. And I expect I'll be all Ezra know because just as sure as shit stank, Rose May ain't went to no hospital. I knew when she left where she was going, but I just wanted to believe she was gonna do right," said Rose, looking so disappointed. "How can a momma not love her children, Tony? How? These babies are her blood. They my blood, and I'll die and go meet the Good Master before I let anything happen to these babies," Rose said while hugging Elijah tightly.

"I know, Grandma Rose," agreed Tony. "I knew when you told me she was gone. What it was," said Tony, reaching to hold Elijah, who was now trying to talk. "I'll be here for you, Grandma Rose, no matter what. We'll get through this. We both love Rose May and the babies. Whatever and whenever you need me, I'll be here," said Tony, almost in tears.

His heart was breaking, not just for himself, but for Grandma Rose and the boys because he knew before it was over they would go through hell and back, dealing with Rose May and her drug addiction.

"Thank you, baby," Rose said as she looked up at Tony, holding Elijah. "I always knew you was a good boy from the first time I met you. You always had a good heart. You would have made a nice mate for Rose May. But that fool will drag you through the mud, Tony," said Rose, shaking her head. "She's blessed to have you in her life and me and the boys are, too," said Rose, looking down. "Now where in the hell is that crazy-ass girl at wit my damn car!" said Rose as she reached up in the cabinet behind the Grandma's Molasses for her "special bottle."

Rose and Bessie had started taking a little shot every now and then. Rose said it helped her to feel better and ease her stress level. The other excuse she used was that it helped her blood. Rose took the glass down, poured a double shot of the Christian Brothers Brandy in the glass and turned it up. *Boy, that felt good*, Rose thought, as the sting of the brandy hit the back of her throat.

"Tony, you all right?" Rose yelled from the kitchen.

"Yes, mam. Me and Lijah just chillin' getting aquainted. Mind if I take him for a walk?" Tony yelled.

"No, baby, go head on. He need the fresh air," Rose yelled back jubilantly.

"Okay, we'll be back," Tony said as he and Elijah exited through the front door.

When Rose heard the door close, she poured another shot. Rose felt warm all over, it felt comforting. Rose's conscience started to talk, *You know you don't need to be drinking! You a churchgoing woman on the usher board*, said the good side. *Aw, shit, go on an' have yo self a drink. Jesus drunk wine in the Bible, and it is called Christian Brothers*, said the bad side. "Shut up!" Rose said as she poured another glass.

"Who you talkin' to?" said Bessie as she entered the kitchen.

"Nobody," said Rose as she turned around quickly. "Get a glass an' have a drink wityo best girlfriend," Rose said, slurring slightly.

"Where Lijah at?" Bessie asked, looking around.

"Tony took him for a little stroll," Rose said, giggling as she poured Bessie a drink.

"All right now, Rose, you soundin' a little tipsy. You know we only use that stuff for our aches and pains," said Bessie, downing her shot in one big gulp.

"Well damn it. I got some aches and pain. Do you know that trifling cow done took my damn car, talking 'bout she going to the hospital. She ain't comin' back, Bessie. She ain't comin' back! I'ma kill that heffer if she make it back here! I can't take this shit no more, Bessie. I got Lijah and another po' sick grandbaby laying up in the hospital, an' a foolish-ass girl out here running after dope. What I'm gone do, Lord? What I'm gone do?" slurred Rose, now with big crocodile tears streaming down her pretty brown cheeks.

"It's gonna be all right, child! The good Lord ain't left you yet, and He ain't gonna leave you now!" Bessie said, now holding her friend up, helping her to the sofa.

Rose was drunk. Rose lay on the couch and passed out. Bessie looked down at her friend, who looked like she had the weight of the world on her shoulders, and covered her up with a blanket. She couldn't help but feel empathy for her best friend because she was in a terrible pickle.

39

When Rose finally cracked her eyes open, she felt the banging in her head. "Lija! Lija! Where Lija at?" she yelled, sitting up, holding her head.

"He all right, Grandma Rose, he all right. He ain't even got up yet. When we got back, Miss Bessie was here. I gave him a bath and put him to bed, and I figured I'd stay here wit y'all, and let Miss Bessie go on home," Tony said with a sad look. "I ain't heard from Rose May, and it's six in the morning. You want me to fix you some coffee?" Tony asked, moving toward the kitchen.

"Yeah, baby, that'll be fine. I'm sorry, Tony. I didn't mean to do that. But Rose May done put so much on me. I sure appreciate you staying here and looking after my baby," Rose said, reaching for a BC Powder on the end table. "I don't know what I'm gonna do Tony. That fool got my car, and she know I need to get around! I got the baby here, and I need to get around! I got this baby here, and I need to check on Ezra! What in the hell is she thinking?" said Rose as she got up to look in on Elijah who was sleeping soundly.

Rose returned to the living room and looked at Tony who had his hands in his head, looking down. "Tony, go on home child. We gon' be fine. I gotta go see lil' Ezzie," said Rose, sipping her coffee.

"Grandma Rose, I'm going home. But I'll be back to take you and Lijah to the hospital, and I'm gonna find yo car today!" said Tony, standing up, heading toward the door as if he was on a mission.

Before Rose could say anything, Tony was gone. Rose went in the kitchen and poured the little bit of Christian Brothers Brandy that was left down the sink. Rose looked up and began to talk to God. "Lord, oh, Lord! It's me, Rose again. Please forgive me, Lord, for not depending on you. I'm sorry, Lord. I'll never put another drink to these lips again! Lord, help me, Lord! You ain't failed me yet, and I ain't gonna fail you. Just gimme strength, Lord. I know I got a long row to hoe, and I can't do it without you, Lord. Help me with these babies, Lord, and please, please look after that foolish girl of mine. Amen." Rose let out a sigh and went to get ready to go to the hospital.

Rose and Elijah had just finished dressing. It was about 10:00 a.m. Tony pulled up and was up to the door in what seemed like a second.

"You ready, Grandma Rose?" Tony yelled as he slipped through the door.

"Yeah, baby. Let me get Lijah's car seat. Oh damn, Rose May got it in the car," said Rose, snapping her fingers.

"That's okay. Just hold him in the back seat," said Tony as he picked up little Lijah, who was babbling and grinning up at Tony as he scooped him up.

As Rose, Tony, and Elijah went up the elevator to the NICU, Rose felt an inner peace. She knew little Ezra was going to be fine; she felt it in her spirit. As Rose entered the NICU, she heard little Ezra's cry. It sounded so pitiful. But Rose promised herself she wouldn't break. The nurse approached Rose with the most comforting smile.

"How is he?" Rose asked with trepidation.

"Oh, little Ezra is just fine," the nurse said, comforting. "He's up to four pounds now, and the doctor is lowering his oxygen intake. He might be going home by next week," said the nurse happily while leading Rose to the tiny bed.

Rose looked down on the tiny swaddled figure who had tube coming from his little nose, and he was trying his best to breathe. "Po' little thing. Can you open your eyes? Grandma Rose is here, and she's gonna love you to pieces. You got a big brother waiting to love you too," said Rose, smiling.

Just then, Ezra cracked open his little eyes, and Rose gasped. "Oh, Lord!" shrieked Rose.

"What's wrong, Ms. Carlisle?" asked the nurse.

Rose patted her chest, cleared her throat, and tried to compose herself. "Oh nothing, honey," Rose stammered. "I'll be back later," Rose said while hurriedly exiting the

NICU. Rose sped past Tony and Elijah who were in the waiting room. "Come on," Rose said.

"What's wrong?" asked Tony, scooping up Elijah. "Is the baby all right?" Tony asked inquisitively.

"Yeah, Yeah, he fine. He might be home next week," Rose said, looking as if she'd seen a ghost.

"Why you looking like that, Grandma Rose?" asked Tony, who was really concerned now.

"I'll tell you when we get to the car," said Rose, almost running. When they got to the car and got in, Rose turned to Tony and said, "That baby is the devil!" said Rose.

"Huh?" Tony said.

"That baby is evil, Tony! I see it in his eyes. His eyes look like they got a flame in them. That's a flame of hell! They greenish blue, Tony, wit a flame in the middle. I tell you that baby is evil!" Rose spilled almost out of breath.

"Grandma Rose, you sure?" asked Tony.

"Hell, yeah, I'm sure. I've seen those eyes before. They look pure evil," said Rose. "Lord, help me that baby is my blood so I can't give up on him. Nothing that bad can come out of Rose May!" said Rose. "Tony, boy, you better get prayed up because we bringing home Rose May's baby," Rose said, looking up to God as they pulled off from the hospital.

40

"Danni, I gotta go," said Rose May, turning up a forty-ounce bottle of Colt 45.

"Shut the hell up! You said that two days ago, bitch, and you still stuck in the same spot, putting yo lighter up." Danni laughed and passed Rose May another hit. "You might as well come an move in wit me, girl. You know we can hold a spot down an' you damn sure done made us some money while you been here. We ain't stopped burning since you walked through the door!" said Danni, firing up another rock and passing the stem to Rose May, who was looking extremely crazy.

"I gotta get my momma car back. I know she trippin'," said Rose May.

"You know it," said Danni. "Girl, I remember the last time Miss Rose caught us smoking in her house before you had the baby," Danni said, picking on the floor. "Girl, yo momma went shell! Miss Rose ain't nothing nice when she pissed off. Please don't tell her where I stay!" Danni said, looking up at Rose May wide-eyed.

"What da hell I'm gonna do," said Rose May. "I gotta get dat damn car home, an I ain't even thought about goin' to see that baby," Rose May said, looking down sorrowfully.

"Why the hell you keep callin' him 'that baby'?" asked Danni. "He yo baby act like you don't even count him," Danni said, still picking on the floor.

"Danni, you know what the hell I went through wit that damn fool, Reno. I don't want nothing reminding me of him. Hell, no I don't want that baby!" said Rose May with a look of fury on her face.

"Well, hell, you can't just erase a baby" said Danni. "Let's just go drop the car off. We ain't gotta go in. You know yo momma gon' take care of that baby. And come on and move in her wit me. Girl, we got it goin' on!" said Danni, twirling around like a cracked-out ballerina.

Rose May looked at Danni and thought to herself, *What the hell. I ain't gon' be shit no way.*

"Come on, let's go drop dis damn car off," said Rose May as she burned her last hit.

41

Another day rolled around, and Rose hadn't gotten any sleep. Rose creeped through the drab apartment, looking dismayed. Elijah was still sleeping. It wasn't even seven o'clock. As Rose put on her morning pot of coffee, she looked out the window.

"What's wrong, Grandma Rose?" said Tony, stumbling to the kitchen. Tony hadn't left Rose's side just as he had promised.

"My car, Tony! My car is out there!" said Rose as she ran and opened the door.

"Is Rose May out there?" asked Tony right on Grandma Rose's heel.

"I don't see her. That damn heffer! She ain't had the decency to come in and say nothing. The fool just ran off! What about the baby! What about the baby!" said Rose, pacing around the car getting wound up.

"Calm down, Grandma Rose, calm down," said Tony, now rummaging through the car as if he was looking for clues.

"Tony, I don't know what I'm gon' do!" said Rose as she went back into the apartment. "This just ain't right. It just ain't right. I got too much on me!" said Rose as she reached in the cabinet. Just as Rose was fumbling through the cabinet for the Christian Brothers Brandy, she stopped and caught herself. "Oh, Lord, what am I doin'? Lord, please forgive me. I know you ain't gon' put more on me than I can bear. Please, Jesus, forgive me," said Rose as she turned away from the cabinet and looked at Tony, who was now holding Elijah. He was now a year old and growing extremely fast. "Well, Tony, I better be getting myself ready to go to the hospital and pick up Ezra. The good thing is I got my car back," said Rose sorrowfully as she retreated to the bathroom to shower and change.

42

The spot was crunk! Rose May had been staying with Danni for about a month now, and they were moving some real weight. Plus, they could smoke all the crack they wanted to. It was Friday and the first of the month! Rose May was feeling real prosperous today. She was expecting to pull in at least a grand. Besides cooking, cutting, and selling dope, Rose May had her regular tricks that paid her well! Rose May hadn't even thought about her family she left behind. That's why she tried to stay high all of the time. Rose May had taken all the skills Aunt Minnie had taught her and put them to good use. She and Danni had the best trap around town.

"Hey, bitch! Where you at?" yelled Danni, walking through the house in nothing but a thong, carrying his stem.

"Back here. Bring me a blast," yelled Rose May as she put on her short shorts.

"Girl, I got a trick up front that wanna holla at you and me, if you know what I mean," said Danni, winking and putting a piece of dope on Rose May's stem.

"How much?" said Rose May as she inhaled the intoxicating smoke and held it in for a few seconds. Rose May felt her eyes vibrating as she let the smoke out.

"Three hundred," said Danni.

"Hell, yeah!" said Rose May, looking high and glassy-eyed. The rock was ruling her. The rock was making her decisions for her. Rose May jumped up, twirled around, and said, "Let's set this bitch off."

Rose May was in rare form tonight. Not only was Rose May full of crack. She had snorted powder, snorted heroine, drank about ten beers, and was working on a fifth of Richards Wild Irish Rose. Rose May was down for anything when the perverted fat baldhead trick requested that Rose May and Danni have sex while he watched.

Rose May stumbled up the hallway to the room where Danni and the fat boy pervert were waiting.

"Drop a boulder," said Rose May as she entered the room, brandishing her stem.

"I know that's right!" said Danni, putting his lighter up.

Before long, the small room was filled with crack smoke, and Danni and Rose May had consummated their deal and pocketed three hundred dollars in the process. This Friday night lasted for about a week. Rose May and Danni hadn't stopped smoking for seven days!

"Rose May, Rose May!" yelled Danni, coming to the back." I'm done. Lock it up. Girl, we ain't had no sleep or nothing. I'm gon' lock it up. I ain't on point I'm gon' putting everybody out!"

Rose May was so high she couldn't respond. All she could do was hold up one finger and blow smoke. Rose May was in a bad, bad, bad, bad situation. She was oblivious to how bad the situation really was.

There was a loud bam at the front door. It was a raid! All Rose May could do was sit there. There were baggies, stems, lighters, crack cans, screen, and everything else illegal you could think of lying around. Rose May and Danni both were carted off to jail for possession and maintaining a dwelling for distribution, not to mention the other charges.

43

It was about 8:00 a.m. when the phone rang. Rose was in a rather good mood, considering her circumstances. Today was the day Ezra was coming home. He had been in the hospital a month and two weeks. Rose had resigned herself to just do the best she could and depend on God whatever would be.

"Hello," Rose answered more cheerful than she really was.

"You have a collect call from the Crenshaw County Jail. Press one to accept and two to decline," said the message.

Rose's fingers were trembling as she reluctantly pressed 1.

"Hey, Ma," said Rose May timidly on the other end.

Rose just held the receiver. She didn't know what emotion she was feeling. Rose didn't know if she was mad, glad, or sad. Her head was spinning. "Rose May, are you all right?" Rose said, cupping the receiver with both hands tightly.

"I'm okay, Ma. The spot I was in got busted, and my bail is twenty-five thousand dollars. All I need is twenty-five hundred dollars to get out," said Rose May almost out of breath.

"Rose May! Where in the hell am I gon' get twenty-five hundred dollars from?" said Rose, getting mad.

"I don't know, Ma. I was jus telling you," said Rose May sorrowfully. "How the baby doin'? What his name again?" said Rose May.

Rose's face screwed up, and she answered angrily, "He's fine! He need his damn momma, and so do Lijah! What in the hell is wrong wityou? I hope this done taught you some sense. Now what you gon' do, Rose May? What you gon' do? Atleast you in jail, and I can get some rest because I know where you are. You about to be the sorriest somebody I ever done seen. I ain't raise you like this, Rose May! These children yo blood, and you don't give a damn!" said Rose, who was now completely wound up.

"I know, Ma. I'm sorry, Ma. Please try and get me out, Ma. I done learned my lesson, Ma. Please!" begged Rose May on the other end.

"I'll see what I can do," said Rose as she hung up the phone. Rose plopped down in her chair and shook her head. "Where in the world am I gone get twenty-five hundred?" she said out loud.

Just as Rose made that statement, Bessie came through the door with Tony trailing behind her.

"Hey, Rose, where the babies at?" said Bessie.

"Morning, Grandma Rose," said Tony, looking at her inquisitively.

"I heard from her y'all," said Rose in a mundane tone.

"You did?" they both said in unison. "Where she at? She all right?" said Tony and Bessie, shouting.

"Yeah, jail. And she need twenty-five hundred for bail," said Rose slowly, looking downward.

"I got some money saved up, Grandma Rose. I'll let you have it," said Tony.

"Tony, I can't let you do that, baby. That's yo money, an' I know you done worked hard for it," said Rose solemnly.

"It's okay, Grandma Rose. Please, you know, I'll do anything for Rose May," pleaded Tony.

"Okay then, Tony. You know you a good friend. You sure have been a blessing to this family," said Rose gratefully.

Rose, Bessie, Tony, and Elijah piled up in Rose's '73 Cadillac Coupe Deville and headed off to the hospital to pick up Ezra. Today was Ezra's homecoming. Even though Rose was feeling weak and bewildered, she knew she had to be strong and focused because she had two demons coming home on the same day.

44

Rose waited anxiously in the long corridor and paced back and forth. She hadn't seen Rose May since she gave birth to Ezra. What would she say? How would she react? Rose didn't know what to feel. Rose had decided to pick up Rose May first and then go to the hospital to get Ezra.

Rose heard the clank of the iron door on the other end of the corridor. When she looked up, her jaw dropped in astonishment. Was that her beautiful girl coming toward her? "No can't be!" said Rose aloud to herself. Rose May looked a mess! As Rose approached Rose May cautiously, she surveyed her from head to toe. Where her hair was once long, thick, beautiful, it was now short and thin. And her beautiful hazel eyes, there were dark circles and bags under them. Rose May's beautiful caramel-colored complexion was now gray and ashen. Where her figure was once voluptuous, she was a now bag of bones. Her cheeks were sunken like deep valleys.

Rose held out her arms and began to weep uncontrollably. "Oh, my po' baby! Look at her, Lord, look at her!" Rose sobbed.

Rose May slid from her mother's tight embrace and began to weep uncontrollably too.

"I'm sorry, Ma. I'm sorry. I done learned my lesson this time, Ma. Thank you, Ma, for getting me," said Rose May with snot running from her nose.

"It's okay, baby. The Lord is good. Now I'm gon' take you and them babies home, and we gon' get on wit life! The good Lord done spared you once again, Rose May! Thank you, Jesus!" Rose shouted, did a little jig, and threw up her hand as they exited the jail.

Tony, Bessie, and Elijah were waiting in the parking lot as Rose and Rose May approached. When Tony looked up and saw Rose May, he didn't see the emaciated, thin-haired, ashen-skinned crackhead she had become; he saw the same chunky schoolgirl he had fallen in love with years ago. Tony's heart was racing. He hadn't seen Rose May since before Elijah was born. God he loved that girl. He didn't know why he still loved her, but he did. And he knew he couldn't just stop.

It was Tony's desire that Rose May would get it together, and they could become a family. Every time Tony tried to court Rose May after a couple of days, she would go off on one of her wild escapades, and he would be left holding his heart in his hand. Nevertheless, Tony refused to give up because he truly believed that love covers a multitude of sins.

"Hey, Tony, Miss Bessie," said Rose May as she approached the car.

"Hey, baby, how you feeling?" said Bessie in a loving sorrowful tone.

"I've seen better days," said Rose May, turning to Tony who was holding Elijah.

"Hey, baby girl, long time no see," said Tony, grinning from ear to ear.

"I know," said Rose May, reaching for Elijah who began to pull away from her as if she were a stranger.

"Aw, Lijah. Now that's yo momma. Don't act like that, baby," said Rose, reaching for him.

Rose May looked down disappointedly.

"It's all right, baby. He just gotta use to ya again," said Rose, stroking Rose May's back.

"Now let's get on to that hospital and get Ezra. Then I'll have all my babies at home wit me. Come on, Bessie. We gon' fry us up some good ol' chicken, make some a yo buttermilk corn bread put on a pot of beans , and some lemonade. My baby need some meat on her bones," said Rose, smiling as they all piled in the Coupe Deville and headed to the hospital.

45

Rose May sat in her room, looking around. *What an idiot*, she thought. *How did my life come to this?* she pondered. Rose May could hear the chicken frying and the pots and pans clanking in the kitchen as she held little Ezra tightly in her arms. She knew her mother was so happy to have her home.

Rose was acting like Rose May came home from the war, not from jail. Rose May felt like she had come home from a war. Rose May stood up and looked at herself in the mirror eye to eye and said out loud, "I'm gon' do it this time. I'm gon' live right and be somebody. I'm gon' raise my boys and make my momma proud." Rose May said that looking down, stroking tenderly little Ezra's cheek.

Rose May had showered and tried to fix herself up as best she could. All of the clothes in her closet were too big. Imagine that! Rose May briefly reflected on her younger years when she was filling out a size 20W. *Where had that innocent, cute, chubby little girl who was full of life and ambition gone? Where was she?* Rose May wondered as she pulled up the baggy size 9 Guess jeans that used to cup her bodacious booty so snuggly. "I look a hot mess!" Rose May said aloud to herself. "Where did all my pretty hair go?" Rose May said as she ran her fingers through her once-thick brown locks.

Just as Rose May was about to start boo hooing over her looks, there was a knock on her door.

"Can I come in?" said Tony, peeping around the door.

"Yeah, why not?" said Rose May sniffing, holding back her tears.

"What's wrong, baby girl?" said Tony, reaching to pull Rose May into his strong loving arms.

"Oh, Tony!" Rose May began falling into Tony's arms, crying as a dam that had burst.

"I look a mess. I got two babies wit' no daddy. I ain't got nothing," Rose May stammered.

"Rosie, Rosie, shh, shh, shh," said Tony soothingly as he placed his fingers over her lips and bent down to kiss her tenderly.

Rose May closed her eyes, and for a moment, she was lost in Tony's tender kiss and embrace.

"Tony, stop. What you doin'?" said Rose May as she turned away and went over to the bed to pick up Ezra, who was sleeping soundly.

"Rose May, you know I love you, girl, and always have since we was kids. I don't care about all the stuff you done. I'll love the boys like they was my own," Tony said, practically pleading with Rose May.

"Tony, look at me. Look what a pickle I'm in. How can you possibly wanna be with me?" asked Rose May, looking confused.

"I love you, girl! That's how!" Tony said, emphatically throwing up his hands. "Are you gon' let me love you, Rose May, and take care of you and the boys?" asked Tony, moving toward Rose May and Ezra.

Just as Rose May was turning to give Tony his answer, they heard, "Y'all come eat! It's ready, Tony, Rose May. Y'all come on before the food get cold!" yelled Grandma Rose.

Rose May turned and gave Tony a shy glance and hurried out of the room with Ezra. Tony just stood there for a few moments and then followed her longingly.

"What took y'all so long? Didn't you hear me callin'?" asked Rose as she lifted Elijah and put him in his high chair. "Bessie, come on. This is a celebration dinner. I got all my babies home wit me. God is a good God," said Rose as she beamed with happiness.

"God sure is good," said Bessie, smiling as she pulled a chair out, sat down, and grabbed a crispy chicken leg.

When everyone was seated, Rose looked over at Rose May and asked, "You wanna say grace, baby?"

"No, Ma. I don't think He'll hear me," Rose May said disappointedly.

"Oh, baby, He'll hear. He done heard you this far. You here, aint' you? Now you thank the Lord. Go on now, Rose May. Go on," said Rose urgingly.

Rose May folded her hands, bowed her head, and began," Dear Lord, I thank you that I'm here tonight and not out high somewhere on the street. I thank you, Lord, for my family and friends and this wonderful meal my momma has prepared for us. In Jesus's name, Amen." Rose May lifted her head and looked up.

"Amen," everyone said in unison.

"Thank you, baby. That was nice, real nice," Rose said, smiling and grabbing the steaming bowl of collard greens.

46

"Rose May, Rose May. Get up! Get up, girl, and see about the baby!" yelled Rose across the hall. "What's wrong wit that boy? He cry all the damn time. It's three in the morning. That baby been crying all night," complained Rose.

"I don't know what's wrong wit him, Ma. He dry, and he ain't hungry," Rose May said as she dragged herself over to the bassinet and picked up Ezra.

Rose May walked and rocked, walked and rocked until finally little Ezzie went to sleep. It was 5:00 a.m. Just as Rose May turned over in a comfortable position, she heard, "Get up, girl. Lijah hungry. These babies are your responsibility. I been doing it by myself long enough. It's time for Grandma to get some rest," said Rose, reaching over and plopping Elijah on the floor.

"Ma, I ain't slept all night. I'm tired," said Rose May, screwing up her face.

"I don't give a damn about that Rose May. Now get yo triflin' ass up and feed this boy!" yelled Rose, sounding as though she was getting wound up.

Rose May got up and went over to pick up Elijah. Elijah looked up at his mother and smiled. Rose May smiled back and said, "You a sweet baby, aint you? Mommy gon' take care of you now," Rose May said, squeezing her baby tightly.

Elijah was a calm baby with a sweet spirit. He never really cried or whined. He was a perfect little gentleman. Elijah looked just like his daddy, the good reverend Jeremiah Jones. Rose May often wondered what had happened to him. She never tried to look him up. As far as the "good reverend" was concerned, Rose May was still waiting by the door with her bags packed. *A sorry bastard*, Rose May thought out loud as she put on a pot of grits for Elijah's breakfast.

Just as Rose May began to stir the grits, Ezra began to cry. She had to make a bottle. Damn, the pot was boiling over. "Ma! Ma! Come help me," Rose May screamed as she tried to make up Ezra's bottle and grab up Elijah at the same time.

Rose heard her, but she was playing possum. Rose turned over and snuggled deeper into her covers with an impish grin on her face.

"Ma! Ma! Please come help me."

Rose just laid there for a minute. "Damn!" Rose said as she slung the covers off and walked to the kitchen. "This damn boy cry too much. It's something wrong wit him," complained Rose as she bent down to pick up Ezra, who was the spitting image of his father. "Look at him, Rose

May. Look at him. Look at his eyes. They evil, just plain evil!" Rose said as she entered the kitchen.

"Aw, Ma. No, he ain't he's a baby," said Rose May, maneuvering Elijah on her hip.

"Yeah, he is. You know what a no-good, lowdown daddy he got. That man ain't shit, and he ain't gon' be shit," announced Rose, attempting to feed Ezra.

"Ma, please," said Rose May, getting a little preturbed, shoveling a hefty spoonful of grits in a bowl to cool for Elijah.

"Please, hell," said Rose. "I don't know what in the hell you meant fooling wit that no-good, no-count Reno James. Everybody know that nigga ain't shit." Rose complained, putting Ezra's bottle down and frowning at him.

"Ma, please, please stop. Now is not the time," Rose May exclaimed as she blew the spoon of grits and attempted to feed Elijah as he sat there like a perfect little gentleman.

"Now that's my boy," Rose said as she beamed at Elijah, and he grinned back.

"Here then. You take him," said Rose May as she pushed the bowl of grits toward her mother and picked up Ezra who was crying.

Grandma Rose said those eyes were just plain evil. But anyone who looked deeply into them would be taken away. They were breathtaking, just like his daddy's. Reno's eyes had a bewitching quality. His son's had the same effect—Ezra had a cute little button nose with the cutest set of plump rosy lips beneath. The only problem was those lips never stayed shut! You could never tell if Ezra was sick, hungry, or needed to be changed because he cried all the time!

As Rose May was sitting in her easy chair holding Ezra, who had just stopped crying, she looked over at Elijah, playing quietly on the floor. Elijah was a good baby, a calm baby. He looked just like his daddy too. Smooth, creamy black skin. Just like a Hershey bar. His hair was black and shiny with tight curls all over his head. Elijah's eyes had a look of great wisdom and strength in them. His smooth little chubby cheeks were pierced with dimples that looked like little ditches on the side of his face. They were always visible because he smiled all the time.

As Rose May was sitting there, rocking Ezra, gazing at Elijah, and reminiscing about Reverend Hershey (whom she still loved), Rose peeped in her door.

"Where you goin', Ma?" Rose May asked with a look of desperation.

"Why?" asked Rose, entering the room, gazing and admiring herself from a full-length mirror head to toe. Rose was wearing a red dress that complemented her figure well. Her red alligator shoes and red alligator bag were the perfect accessories. Rose's hair was still beautiful. It fell softly over her brow and rested a little beneath her shoulders. Rose was still a knockout.

Rose May looked up at her mother jealously and asked again, "Where you goin'?"

"I'm goin' out, Rose May. I ain't got no children, and I'm still a young, good-looking woman," Rose said as she turned around to look at her firm backside and grinned with her perfectly shaped ruby red lips.

"Who you supposed to be going out with?" Rose May asked clearly with an attitude. "I hope it ain't one of them no-count deacons you and Miss Bessie be fooling wit at that church," Rose May said, walking off to the bed to lay Ezra down and pick up Elijah, who was trying to talk now.

Rose snapped her neck around and said, "I'm yo momma, girl, and you ain't got a damn thing to do wit' who I see. I ain't have a damn thing to do wit them trifling niggas you was wit. Now mind your damn business. I'll be home by ten!"

Rose May stood there holding Elijah, rolling her eyes at the doorway her mother had just exited.

"Ummmm hmmmm," Rose said under her breath as she watched the tall brown thick framed man walk through the double doors of the restaurant. As the chocolate dreamboat approached, Rose couldn't help but smile. It felt good to be out on a date after so many years, bottles, diapers, and Rose May.

Boaz. Boaz Brown was his name. Rose had met Boaz at a church singing one night with Bessie. Rose and Bessie were sitting on the front row and Rose noticed Deacon

Brown staring at her from the Deacon's corner. After church he approached her, asked her out, and the rest was history. That was two months ago. Rose felt silly. She was slipping and sneaking around meeting and talking to Boaz in clandestine places. Rose didn't want Rose May or Bessie all in her business. She had pretty much put the responsibilities of the babies on Rose May. After all, she was their mother and she was doing a pretty good job. Well, why did she feel so guilty?

As soon as Rose smelled the pungent aroma of the cologne, she looked up and saw those pretty white teeth between a set of the most perfect lips she had ever seen, her guilt was pushed to the side.

"Hey, Rosie, baby," said Boaz, reaching down to give Rose a lingering peck on the cheek.

"Hey, BB," Rose replied, grinning from ear to ear.

"A rose for my Rosie," said Boaz, handing Rose a beautiful red rose he had hidden behind his back.

"Thank you, Rose said grinning coyly.

"Rose, you look stunning," he said, slipping into the booth beside her.

Rose felt great! And she knew she was looking good. Rose and Boaz laughed and talked through their whole meal. She felt as though she had known Boaz for years.

Boaz Brown was well-established in the community. Boaz had been a widow since the age of thirty-five. His wife died of cancer, and he hadn't remarried, and he didn't have children. Boaz had been going to Mount Jubilee Missionary Baptist Church since he was a child, but Rose hadn't ever noticed him before. Boaz had seen Rose on several occasions, but he didn't have the nerve to talk to her until the second Sunday singing.

Boaz had repeatedly told Rose that the Lord had finally sent him an angel from heaven. Rose blushed uncontrollably every time he told her that. She felt like a silly schoolgirl.

"Rosie, baby, when are you gonna let me meet the family?" Boaz urged.

"Soon, BB, soon. It ain't time yet. I'm trying to let Rose May get settled with the babies first before I spring this on her. She's never known me to have a boyfriend. She might act a fool," Rose said, frowning.

"Okay, baby, I'll be patient. You just let me know when," Boaz said with a confident grin. "Rosie, you wanna go back to my place? We can watch a movie or something," Boaz asked with a seductive grin.

"Boy, you know if I go back to yo place, we ain't gon' watch no movie. Beside, I need to check on the children," Rose said, sliding out of the booth.

Boaz left a generous tip on the table and trailed after Rose as if in a trance. Rose turned to Boaz when they were outside the restaurant and said, "Thanks for the dinner, BB. I'll call you."

"Rosie, baby, are you sure you won't come by just for a while?" Boaz pleaded, stroking Rose's forearm.

"Not now, boy. I gotta go check on the children," Rose said, reaching up to place a big kiss on Boaz's full, round lips.

"Okay, okay, okay. Just don't make me wait too long, Rosie," Boaz said as Rose got in her car.

As Rose drove home to the smooth sounds of Luther Vandross crooning in her ear from the radio, she felt like a million bucks. Rose thought to herself, *Could Boaz be the one?* He sure did feel like the one. Rose had decided that she would invite him to dinner on Sunday.

47

It was Saturday morning, and Rose was up early, cleaning. Boaz was coming to dinner on Sunday, and she wanted everything just right. Rose was rolling her hips and singing an extra soulful version of Betty Wright's "Clean up Woman" while scrubbing the stove.

When Rose May walked in holding Ezra, who was crying as usual, she asked clearly with an attitude, "What you so happy about? Is it because that man is coming to dinner?"

Rose stopped her hips, cut her song off, turned from cleaning the stove, looked Rose May dead in the eye, and said, "Now, Rose May! Don't start no damn shit! You better be on your best behavior. That man has a name. Mr. Boaz Brown!" Rose said, snapping her fingers and storming off.

Rose May rolled her eyes and continued to feed Ezra.

Rose was feeling real crazy today. She didn't know why Rose May hadn't done any drugs or had anything to drink since she'd gotten out of jail. That had been two months ago. Rose May and Tony had been dating since she got home. Rose May loved Tony, but not like Tony loved her. Tony was just too good to her. Rose May just couldn't accept his good treatment for her and the boys. Tony was a good man, as Grandma Rose would say, "A good sturdy working man. With benefits." Every Friday when Tony got paid, he would be right there with check in hand to give Rose May and the boys their weekly allowances. Tony kept Rose May and the boys dressed fine as a fiddle. Rose May didn't have to ask for a thing. Tony's and Rose May's relationship was definitely one-sided. Tony did all he could to win Rose May's heart, but she just wouldn't love him like he loved her.

Rose was dusting the living room when she heard the sound of someone throwing up in the bathroom.

"Rose May, Rose May! What's wrong with you?" Rose asked, dropping her dustrag on the couch, heading for the open bathroom door.

"Yeah, Momma," Rose May said wearily, hugging the toilet.

"Ohhhh hell, naw! Yo period been on? When have you had yo period, Rose May?" Rose was getting wound up. "When, Rose May? When!" Rose screamed.

Rose May looked up at her mom timidly and said, "I don't know."

"What in the hell do you mean you don't know? Rose May Carlisle, I know yo dumbass ain't sitting up here big again. I will beat the hell outa you girl." Rose ranted.

"Ma, I'm probably just late," Rose May said, getting up going to the sink to splash water in her face. Rose just stood there, looking at Rose May like she could strangle her. Rose May looked up at her mother trying not to look nervous. She knew her mother could look in her eyes and read her.

"You better be late. We can't handle that you don't need anymore children, Rose May. Now I ain't got time to deal wit this. I gotta get the food ready for my company," Rose said, rolling her eyes, walking off.

Rose May went to her room, flopped on the bed, and began to cry. She knew. She knew the feeling oh too well. She knew she was pregnant, and she knew her new baby's daddy was a cross-dressing homosexual.

48

It was Sunday morning, and Rose was scurrying around, putting the finishing touches on her dinner, and getting ready for church at the same time.

"Rose May, get on up now and get those children and yourself ready! Make haste. I don't wanna be late!" Rose yelled out while seasoning her big pot of pinto beans.

"I ain't going this morning, Ma. I don't feel good," Rose May yelled back with her head still under the covers.

Rose put the lid on her pot of beans and started down the hall with a frown on her face.

"Rose May, don't start this damn shit this morning. You know how important this dinner is. Now get up and get those babies ready, and I mean now!" Rose yelled, snatching the cover off Rose May.

"Yo period came on yet?" Rose asked, looking at Rose May sideways.

"Not yet, Ma. But I know it is." Rose May lied on.

"You sure better hope it does!" Rose said upon exiting the room.

Rose May felt like crap. She definitely didn't feel like going to old fake Mount Jubilee Missionary Baptist Church, and she wasn't going this morning. She didn't care what her mother said. Rose May did get up and get the boys dressed. She knew her mother would take them. That would give her some free time for herself. Rose May heard her mother's heels clicking coming down the hall.

"You ain't ready?" Rose asked, frowning.

"No, Ma. I ain't going. I don't feel like fooling wit them old fake church folks," Rose May said as she lit up a Newport 100.

"Put that cigarette out you know that smoke ain't good for the babies!" Rose said, snatching the freshly lit cigarette from Rose May's lips. "Well go on and put the car seats in the car. You can stay here and finish my dinner," Rose said, looking at herself up and down in the full-length mirror, smiling.

Rose did look good. She had on a snug-fitting lavender suit with the shoes, pocketbook, and hat to match. Rose definitely didn't look like a grandmother.

"You look real nice, Ma," Rose May said while strapping Ezra, who was still sleeping in his carrier. Elijah was ready too, sitting on the bed like a perfect little gentleman.

"Oooh, look at my babies. They so fine. Come on, Rose May, hurry. I don't wanna be late," Rose said, grabbing her Bible on the way out while giving Rose May instructions on finishing up her dinner.

Rose May stood in the doorway, watching as they pulled off. "What in the hell am I gone do?" she said aloud.

Rose May knew she was in a pickle. What in the world was she gonna do with another baby? Ezra was only five months old, and Elijah was one. *I need a drink*, Rose May thought. Rose May slipped on her sweat suit; checked the pots, the stove; and headed to the liquor house.

49

Rose was feeling good on her way home from church. She peeped up at her rearview mirror and gazed lovingly at the boys sleeping peacefully in the back seat. Rose checked her watch. It was almost two-thirty. Rose hoped Rose May had finished up her dinner because Boaz would be there around three.

As Rose pulled up in front of the apartment, she noticed that the front door was open, and she could hear music thumping. Rose grabbed up the babies from the back seat and headed up the walkway with a frown. Rose flew the door open.

"What the hell!" Rose said, out of breath.

"Oh heyyyyyy, Ma." Rose May slurred, holding her glass of gin up, as if making a toast.

"I know yo ass ain't up in here drunk," Rose said, putting the babies down, moving toward Rose May, who was backing up. "You smell like a damn still. You been over at that liquor house, ain't you? An' you couldn't take yo trifling sorry ass to church. You better be finised with my dinner.

You know my company gonna be here soon. I'm tired of your shit, Rose May, you just won't do right!" Rose said, getting wound up, walking through the kitchen, checking her pots.

Rose May just sat there, grinning. She was drunk and didn't really care what her mother was saying.

"How was churrrch?" Rose May slurred, stumbling while trying to stand.

Rose came from the kitchen and shot Rose May a mean squinty-eyed glance.

"Why? You should have brought yo trifling ass on! Atleast you did finish up my dinner. Now, Rose May, go on and lay it down becasuse my company is gonna be here soon and I don't want no shit," Rose said, sternly pushing Rose May to the back.

As Rose headed back up the hallway, the doorbell rang. "Damn!" Rose said, wiping her hands on her apron. "He's early," Rose said.

Rose opened the door, and there stood Tony. "Hey, baby, I sure am glad to see you. Can you please take Rose May and the boys in her room? She's dead drunk, and I got company coming, Rose said, practically begging Tony.

"Yes, mam," Tony said, heading toward Rose May's room.

Tony opened the door and saw Rose May sprawled out on the bed. She had passed out. *She sure is pretty*, Tony thought to himself, *even in her drunken state*. Tony reached down to stroke her cheek.

"Rosie, Rosie, baby, come on. Get up. I'm taking you and the boys wit me. Come on now. Get up!" Tony begged.

Rose May sat up, weaving from side to side. "Hey, baby, when did you get here? Gimme a kiss." Rose May slurred, holding Tony tight around the neck, puckering up.

"No, Rosie. Come on now." Tony snapped, gathering Elijah and Ezra's bags. Rose May flopped down on the bed and started to cry really hard. "Come on, Rosie. Now you just drunk," Tony said.

"I ain't just drunk, Tony. You just don't know everything is all messed up! I done messed up everything!" Rose May continued sobbing uncontrollably.

"What you talking about, Rosie? Come on now," Tony said, grabbing Rose May by her waist, leading her out of her room and down the hall.

Rose was standing at the end of the hall with her hands on her hips, shaking her head in disgust. "Take her, Tony, before I slap her drunk face," Rose said, looking as if steam was coming from her ears.

"Yes, mam," Tony said, heading out the door. Just as Tony and Rose May hit the first step, Tony looked up and saw a fine-dressed man coming up the walkway. As they met each other, Tony greeted the gentleman, and Rose May peeped at him through her drunken eyes.

As the finely dressed man passed, Rose May said, "Hey, I know him. I know him."

"Come on, girl. That's yo momma's date. You don't know him," Tony said, placing Rose May in the front seat, backling her in. Tony went back in the house to get the babies.

"Tony, this is Mr. Boaz Brown," Rose said, introducing the two gentlemen when Tony came back in to get the babies.

"Nice to meet you, sir," Tony said, extending his hand.

"Likewise," Boaz said.

"Have a seat, Boaz. Make yourself comfortable. Dinner will be ready soon," Rose exclaimed, following Tony to the back to retrieve Elijah and Ezra who were still sleeping.

"Tony, thank you, baby. I don't know what got into that crazy girl this morning!" Rose said, fluffing up her hair in the mirror.

"Rose May been acting real crazy for the last couple a weeks," Tony said, scooping up Elijah in his arms and picking up Ezra in his carrier. "I'll call you later, Grandma Rose," Tony said, exiting.

Rose took a deep breath and smoothed her clothes out. Rose was excited about the fine Mr. Boaz Brown she had been waiting on her front room, but she couldn't ignore the grumble in the pit of her stomach. Something wasn't right.

50

The grumble that Rose had in her stomach was right on point. Rose May was pregnant again. Three months pregnant, to be exact. Rose had been so engrossed in her whirlwind romance with Boaz that she hadn't even noticed Rose May's belly getting rounder and rounder. She had completely forgotten to keep track of her monthly period.

As Rose sat in her easy chair, nursing her glass of Christian Brothers, she couldn't help but wonder where she had gone wrong.

Rose May and the boys were out with Tony, and Rose just happened to be putting clothes away and saw the papers that confirmed how far along Rose May's pregnancy was. Rose was absolutely devastated she didn't know whether to be mad, sad, or glad. At least, Tony would be a good father and husband who loved Rose May and the boys.

As Rose sat there listening to Dorothy Moore crooning the mellow sounds of "Misty Blue," she was feeling Christian Brothers kick in and began to sob uncontrollably.

Rose was crying so hard and loud she hadn't even heard Rose May, Tony, and the boys come in.

"What's wrong, Ma?" Rose May said as she bent down.

When Rose looked up with her puffy red eyes at Rose May, Rose May knew that she knew. Rose May backed up slowly and began to plead.

"Ma, please. Ma, please!" Rose May begged.

Rose stood up, smoothed out her tear-stained blouse, walked over to her door, opened it, and beckoned for Rose May to leave. It was as if she was in a trance. Rose was hurt—hurt down to the bone.

Rose May left out the room as ordered, not knowing what to think or what to say to Tony, who was in the front room waiting for an explanation.

"What's wrong?" Tony asked.

"She knows," Rose May said. "Tony, she knows. She didn't say it, but I know she knows," Rose May said, pacing the floor, wringing her now-sweating hands.

"Rose May, I told you we should've told her," said Tony while putting Ezra down next to Elijah, who was sleeping soundly on the couch.

Rose May snapped her neck around and gave Tony a glance that could've cut right through him.

"Tony, you know good and damn well I wasn't gon' tell her. Least not right now! This the first time she been happy for a long time!" said Rose May, sitting down in a huff.

"Well, she found out anyway, and it's worse because you didn't tell her," Tony snapped. Tony was clearly getting agitated. Tony wanted to tell Rose as soon as Rose May told him. He was happy, happy to be a father, and anticipated becoming a husband.

"Screw you!" Rose May snapped.

"Me and everybody else!" Tony yelled.

"You get the hell out my face, Tony!" Rose May screamed, jumping up.

"I'll get the hell out yo face and yo life," Tony replied with his face all screwed up. "I'm tired of yo shit! I do all I can for you, Rose May, an' you don't appreciate a damn thing. I'm tired of you treating me like a dog. You taking my love for granted!" Tony yelled, turning toward the door, sweat accumulating on his brow.

Rose May would not back down. She looked as if steam were coming from her ears.

"I'm done! It's over, Tony. Get the hell on!" Rose May yelled, pointing to the front door.

By now, both the babies had begun crying. Everything was in an uproar.

Tony turned to leave but not before announcing, "It ain't never gon' be over between us. You got my baby in you!" he said and slammed the door.

Rose May thought, *That's what yo dumbass think.* Rose May knew that the baby growing inside her wasn't Tony's but, as far as she was concerned, that was going to be between her and God.

51

Things were silent around the house for the next few weeks. Rose and Rose May barely spoke to one another. Rose hadn't breathed a word about the new bundle of hell on the way. She had begun to put much of her focus on Boaz.

Rose May and the boys had practically moved in with Tony. So she didn't see much of the budding romance.

Rose had become absolutely gaga over Boaz. The majority of her time was being spent with him.

It was Saturday night, and Rose was getting ready for her standing date with Boaz. Every Saturday night, he took her to the Blue Lagoon, a cozy little bar tucked away in the red light district of town. Rose didn't understand why Boaz loved this little dumpy bar so much. She really didn't care as long as she was with her precious BB.

As Rose sat in front of her mirror applying her makeup, she couldn't help but think about her poor lost seed, Rose May. She knew she had to talk to her eventually, and she sure did miss the boys. Rose knew she couldn't continue to live in this fantasy land with Boaz, pretending everything was lovely when she was really in a pickle.

Rose zeroed her attention on the back corner cabinet over the stove. A tiny voice echoed, *Christian Brothers.* Rose's throat squeezed out a dry gulp as she rubbed her now-sweaty fingertips across her parched throat.

Rose moved like a robot toward the kitchen cabinet. Rose got up on her toes like a prima ballerina and reached in the far right corner for the full bottle. Rose hadn't had a drink for at least a month, and she was doing good. She felt heavy right now, and she needed something right now! Right now! Right now! A soft voice squeezed out, *Wait on me, Rose.* But the banging in her head drowned it out.

Rose felt the warm liquid sting the back of her throat. Rose let out a deep sigh and poured a double. Before reaching for the glass, she thought to herself, *Is this how my baby feels?* Rose shook her head, downed the glass, flipped on Luther Vandross's "A House Is Not a Home" and thought about the fine man she had waiting on her. Whatever pain she had been feeling melted away like snow in springtime.

As Rose swayed back and forth to Luther's smooth crooning that creeped from the cassette deck. She looked down at her feet, snapped back to present time and realized she was swaying, grooving, and sipping her brandy, still in her stockings, panties, and bra. Rose slammed her empty glass on the end table and sprinted to the bedroom to resume dressing for her serious date.

Rose slipped into her slinky little black dress, stepped in her black sling back pumps, gave two quick squirts of Chanel No 5 behind her ears, fluffed her hair, stepped back, did a quick survey of her reflection in the mirror, picked up her keys and bag, and sprinted out the front door.

While sitting in the car, Rose looked up toward heaven and really tried to convince herself that everything was good. As she cranked the car and drove off, she thought of Boaz and how strong and safe his big arms felt around her. There was that voice again, *Wait on me, Rose.* Rose ignored the voice and thought, *Why do I always have to go to him? And why do I feel that grumble in my stomach again?*

Rose May was going absolutely batty at Tony's house. She was twisting her hair, biting her nails, and, more than anything, she was feening for some dope. Scotty was calling her. As Rose May sat on the crumpled-up bed in the hot stuffy bedroom, she thought to herself, *What in the hell was I thinking? Moving in with Tony and his momma! Her mean fat ass.*

Rose May knew Tony's momma didn't like her at all. She always told Tony, "That gal ain't nothing. She ain't come from nothing, and she ain't gon' be nothing. She just like her old Aunt Minnie. Minnie treated po' Mookie like a dog, and she'll do you the same way!"

Tony would always rush to her defense, confessing his undying love.

"Love?" his mamma would say. "She love you and any other man that got some money!"

Rose May didn't give a damn about her or her stupid-ass son right now. Tony was good, too damn good. He was just too good. He was just too perfect. Something wasn't right, and Rose May knew it. She just pushed the feeling under the rug, along with every other painful feeling that overloaded her. Not to mention this faggot-ass baby she was carrying.

Rose May screamed aloud in her head. Something had to give. She felt like she was losing her mind. Tony was constantly nagging her for sex, his dumbass friends were always coming over, and his mother! Miss Mamie Lou Jay! She didn't want Rose May to touch or use anything in her big funky old house! Rose May couldn't even boil a hot dog; she couldn't cook a thing in her funky old kitchen. She really didn't want to. Did Tony really think she would consent to her name being Mrs. Rose May Jay? Heeeell naw! The boys…The boys were a whole different argument. Miss Mamie couldn't understand why Tony wanted to take care of not just another man's baby, but two other men's babies. She definitely didn't believe the baby Rose May was carrying was from her son.

What a relief! Elijah and Ezra were sleep. Rose May felt like a prisoner, locked up with her babies all day. They stayed in the room all day while Tony was working. Tony had stocked the room up with plenty of goodies, everything Rose May and the boys needed. She and Tony had a king-sized bed with big comfy pillows. She could lie down and watch from a fifty-inch screen cable TV with VCR. There was private telephone line and private bath. Elijah and Ezra had their own beds too. They even had a fridge and microwave in the room.

Rose May had been pressuring Tony! Since the end of her first week moving in, Rose May had been telling, urging, even giving him more sex, which was one step up from nothing to move. They needed to get out of big, fat, mean, bossy, always-in-somebody's-business Mamie Lou Jay's house!

Tony would always say, "I know, I know, baby. Let me build on this nest egg a little longer." Punk-ass!" Rose May thought her brow twisted. Tony just wanna hide behind her big nasty dress tail!"

Tony always had been a mama's boy.

Rose May looked down at the watch Tony had just bought her. The long hand was on twelve, and the short hand was on nine.

Nine! Rose May shrieked inside her head. What in the hell was she going to do for eight hours?

Rose May plopped down in the big cushy chair Tony had bought just for her. *Everything was just for you and the boys, Rosie, baby. I love you, Rosie. I love the boys. What you need, what you want, let me get it, let me do it*—"Just shut up!" Rose May said out loud. Ezra began to wail. Rose May popped up and hurried to pick up Ezra. Ezra screamed louder. The more she rocked, the more he cried. "Sshhh, please, Ezzie, please!"

Knock, knock, knock—"Shut that damn baby up! Cry all the damn time! It's something wrong wit dat little green-eyed bastard!" *Slam!*

Rose May heard Mamie's voice trail down the hall before she slammed the door. "That mean old bitch!" Rose May spat as she continued to rock Ezra, who had quieted down. Now Elijah had popped his little black head up. Rose May couldn't complain about Elijah. He was a good baby, so much like her mother. *Momma*, Rose May thought. She missed her momma. She didn't realize how good she had it until she moved here. Rose May looked over at the phone. She wanted to call Rose. She longed to hear her say, "Every thing gon' be all right. Just trust the Good Master. He'll see us thru." Her stomach ached for some of her mother's good old fried chicken and homemade lemonade. She hadn't heard from Rose in a month. *That nigga*, Rose May thought to herself. She was always talking to Rose May about getting lost in a man. And there she was, head all screwed up behind a man!

Rose May changed her mind about making the phone call; put down Ezra, who had resumed napping; and scooped up Elijah.

Elijah looked up at his mother and began to babble. Rose May looked into his dark intense eyes and saw such a look of peace. It was like Elijah was someone else. At that moment, Rose May felt as if she were wrapped in a warm, calming embrace.

Ring! Ring! The phone broke her embrace and her calmness.

"Hello," Rose May said, clearly agitated.

"Hey, Rosie, baby, what you doin'?" Tony sang on the other end.

Rose May's eyes rolled to the top of her head, and before she answered, she thought, *This henpecked nigga.* "Nothin'!" Rose May huffed. "Nothin' at all, Tony. What the hell could I possibly be doing besides sitting my big pregnant ass in this damn room with these damn babies, listening to yo fat-ass momma talk shit!" Rose May snapped.

"What's wrong now, Rosie? You need anything? The boys okay? What momma done said now?" Tony rattled. "I'll be home on my lunch break. Gotta go!" *Click.*

Rose May just stood there, holding Elijah, dumbfounded. She looked around at what was once her safe haven. It had now become her prison.

Rose drove home, still enveloped with the scent and passion of Boaz. Rose's head was reeling. She still hadn't distinguished whether it was her passion-filled night or her three double shots of tequila, which had her head rocking.

Rose hadn't had many nights like the one she had just left behind. The only man she had ever known was Rose May's daddy, and she was just a kid then. Rose hadn't had many dates over the years. Her time was spent on working and what she thought was loving Rose May.

As the morning sun pierced through the windshield, Rose began to replay the night of passion she had just spent with Deacon Brown.

Rose was already a little tipsy when she arrived at Boaz's house, and he really tried to make a good impression.

Boaz had tried to prepare a romantic meal of Stouffer's lasagna is considered romantic. He had the music, candles, and everything that went along with being-a-romantic package.

Rose rewound the tape in her mind over and over again. She couldn't really remember much after the tall blue cocktail Boaz fixed her. She did remember the feeling of waking up with a big fine man next to her. Still from the tall blue cocktail, waking up this morning, she found everything really fuzzy.

Rose's look of bewilderment was soon replaced with a look of sheer ecstasy as she fast-forwarded the tape in her mind to waking up cuddled in Boaz's big wide arms.

Rose hadn't bothered to wake Boaz when she left. To tell the truth, she was actually a little ashamed. Rose had always been a very modest woman, and she couldn't stand the thought of not remembering everything she had done. Had she really drank that much?

Rose pulled up the drive and stopped abruptly. Rose looked down at her thigh. How in the world had she gotten such a bruise? Just as Rose exited the car, there stood Bessie, grinning.

"Oooh, child, look like somebody done did something. Tell me all about it. I'm gon' put us on a fresh pot," Bessie said, running breathlessly toward Rose.

"Bessie, it really ain't much to tell," Rose said, opening the front door, trying to block Bessie, who just burst through the flimsy blockade.

"Come on in," Bessie said, reaching for the coffee. "You know you got some business. You ain't been here all night. I know you done broke that fine Deacon Boaz Brown off! I know it!" Bessie roared, slapping her hip.

Rose just dropped her head shamefully, almost in tears.

"What's wrong, girl? You sure ain't actin' like a woman who was just laid up wit one of Mount Jubilee Missionary Baptist's finest deacons!"

"It just don't feel right, Bessie. Something just ain't right." Rose stammered, pacing the floor.

"What you mean?" Bessie asked.

"I mean, I don't like myself, Bessie. I don't think about the same things. I don't do the same things, and I have been drinking a little more."

"Well, Rose, you got a man now. It ain't just you no more. Rose May done gone on and she got her children. It's time for you to live now. Shoooot, I wish I had me a fine deacon. I'd be around here skipping!" Bessie said covetously.

"And Rose May. That's something else I been pushing out my mind, Bessie. That's my child. And the boys…and she got another one on the way," Rose lamented as she dropped her head.

Bessie's neck looked as if it would snap off she turned it so fast.

"Another one? When? By who? Tony? Why you didn't tell me, Rose? Po', child! Po', child! What she gon' do? What you gon' do?" Bessie spewed.

"I need to call her," Rose solemnly stated. "I need to call that fool!"

Just as Rose reached for the phone, it rang.

"Hey, Rosie, baby, I woke up, and you were gone. I'd planned on a little breakfast in bed, if you know what I mean," the sly, husky voice spilled over phone.

Rose just cradled the receiver for a moment. "Yeah, uh, let me call you back. Okay?" Rose shamefully replied.

"Okay, baby. Is everything okay?"

"Yeah, everything's fine. I'll call you." Rose hung the phone up and returned her attention to Bessie, who was listening like a hungry wolf.

Rose just wanted to be alone right now. She felt like nobody could possibly understand how she was feeling right now, and she certainly wasn't going to try and explain it to Bessie. Bessie would have been happy to have Snoopy lying next to her.

Rose kindly escorted Bessie to the door and showed her out, only after promising to call.

Rose showered, changed, and checked her answering machine. Not one. Not one single call from Rose May.

Rose plopped down in her easy chair and pondered the events that had taken place over the last month.

Her daughter, the only child she would ever have, had two children and one on the way—all three with different daddies. She hadn't heard a thing from her in over a month. She was shacked up, living in sin with old henpecked Tony at his momma's house. *I know Rose May is going crazy*, Rose thought. *Three grandchildren. I have three grandchildren. How is this going to play out? It was all becoming too heavy.* Rose sat up. Her head was really beginning to hurt. *Boaz, Boaz Brown*, Rose pondered. *What in the hell am I doing? I know I don't need to be laying up wit no man, especially right now.* Something was missing. Rose felt like she was forgetting something as she stood in the middle of the floor, rubbing her head.

Just as she was about to reach for her "special bottle," she felt that all-too-familiar grumble in her stomach. Was it something or someone Rose was missing?

Boaz sat straight up on the side of his bed and scratched his aching temple. He wondered why Rose had been so curt. Maybe she knew something. He thought he'd fixed her Blue Motorcycle just right. Boaz opened his night stand drawer and surveyed the bevy of pornographic snapshots he had collected over the past several months.

Boaz reached under the corner of his mattress and stared lustfully at Rose's provocative photos.

What a nice one, Boaz thought, beginning to rub himself.

Boaz's intentions for Rose were far more than just a quick fling. Boaz thought Rose was a keeper. She was a fine-looking woman with nice ass, nice boobs, and to top it off, she was twelve years his junior.

"Yeah," Boaz said aloud. "I can mold her like I want her."

Another thing Boaz liked was that Rose was a church girl. She felt like a virgin. He knew Rose would be willing and more than able to take care of him. He'd heard about the nice "lump sum" Rose had gotten when her uncle passed a few years ago.

They'd make a good church couple. With Rose on his arm, nobody would ever suspect Boaz's perverted lifestyle.

Boaz sat up and thought of the trail of torn-up emotions he'd left behind, men and women.

After Boaz's wife died, he began to experiment. Boaz had developed a pension for prostitutes and kinky sex.

So many women, so many men, so many sleazy motels—
and the money, so much money. Boaz was almost tapped
out. Rose came along at the perfect time. He would have
his freak with him at all times, even at church.

It was time for him to settle down, and Rose was
the ticket.

Boaz stood up, lit a KOOL, walked over to his fully
stocked closet, and proceeded to pick out one of his many
sharp suits. He had a deacons' board meeting this morning.

Tony burst through the door, bearing gifts as usual. Rose
May rolled her eyes as hard as she could.

"Hey, baby!" Tony sang joyously. That's what made Rose
May madder than anything. What in the hell was he so
damned happy about?

"Shhhhhhh!" Rose May spat. "I just got these damn
babies to sleep!"

"Ouch, sorry, baby. You miss me today? I brought y'all
something," Tony whispered, holding out the packages.
Rose May grimaced.

"What's wrong, baby? I got you them shoes you wanted,"
Tony pleaded.

Rose May turned to Tony, walked toward him, and
slapped his face really hard.

"You punk-ass bitch! Do you think some damn shoes is
going help this situation? You need to get yo faggot ass up

and out yo momma's house. I can't take this shit no more, Tony. Either you get us a place, or I'm leaving, and that's the bottom line!"

Tony just stood there, his face still stinging from the fiery blow.

"Rosie, baby, now don't get yourself all worked up. Remember our baby!"

Rose May got so mad she saw stars.

"Our baby!" Rose May spewed.

Just then, Elijah and Ezra woke, with Ezra screaming as usual. *Bam! Bam! Bam!* "Tony! Shut them damn chaps up now!"

"Okay, Ma, okay, Ma," Tony timidly replied through the door.

Rose May was seething with anger. The fury Tony saw illuminated her twisted face. Tony had to think quick because he knew Rose May was about to blow.

"Here, baby, here…," Tony said, reaching in his front pocket. "Take this money, take the keys, and go out for a little while."

Rose May's anger was squelched when her eyes zeroed in on the wad of cash Tony pulled out of his pocket.

Rose May didn't utter a word. She grabbed the cash, keys her purse, and headed for the door.

As soon as the bedroom door slammed behind, there was a trail of Rose May's Chanel N°5. Tony felt a pang of fear go through his body as he stood there, holding Ezra in his arms. He looked down at Elijah, who was gripping his pant leg, and he knew from the look of intensity and wisdom in Elijah's eyes that he had just taken a wrong turn.

Rose May peeked at the dashboard. She was doing 60 in a 45. She'd better slow down, she thought to herself.

Rose May knew exactly where she was headed. She didn't have to even give it a second thought.

She was on her way to see her baby daddy, or was it baby mama?

Rose May pulled up to Danyales on two wheels. She hadn't even bothered to look at the wad of cash Tony had given her. She fished the cash out of her bra, and when she looked at the seven $20 bills and the two $50 bills, her stomach did a dive. She knew it wasn't the baby inside her because she hadn't felt that little bastard move in weeks, and she didn't care.

Rose May tucked the bills back in her bra as she leapt up the front stairs.

Knock, knock, knock—Rose May was shifting back and forth, side to side. Her hands were sweating, head pounding. She felt like she had to throw up right now! Right now!

The front door swung open, and there stood her baby daddy/momma in a slinky silk robe with a pair of heels on.

"Heey, bitch! Where you been? You pregnant again?"

Rose May pushed past the RuPaul look-alike and said, "I'm sick."

"I got just the thing for you!" Danni dropped a fifty-dollar piece of crack in Rose May's outstretched sweaty hand. She felt her knees buckle.

"Gimme a shooter!" Rose May said in a dry whisper.

"Coming right up," Danni said.

Rose May extended her shaky hand to retrieve the already loaded shooter. Rose May broke a big chunk of dope, packed it in the back end of the shooter, snapped her fingers repeatedly, and Danyale passed her a BIC lighter.

Rose May flicked her BIC, put the shooter to her trembling lips, guided the flame to the end of the shooter; and when she heard the dope frying like bacon, she closed her eyes, inhaled, and lifted off. When Rose May opened her eyes, they were vibrating. She couldn't talk. She just stood there, holding the smoking hot pipe.

"Heeeelll yeah! I got that fire!"

"I sure am glad to see you. You know I wanted to look you up, but I'm scared of yo, momma! Miss Rose know she hate me!"

Rose May was stuck. She saw Danni's lips moving but couldn't hear a word past the vibration in her head.

This was the feeling she was looking for. She was there. She didn't give a damn what Danni was saying. She wanted to keep this feeling going. They could catch up on old times later.

Rose May dug in her bra and pulled out her wad of cash. The sight of the wad stopped Danni's line of questioning. "Oohh, bitch, you straight! Come on, let's go to Scotty," Danni said, leading Rose May to the back room, which was commonly known as the upper room.

"Let's go to the upper room, honey!" Rose May followed Danyales's scantily clad body down the hall. As the door closed, Rose May's mind closed too. At this point in the game, nothing mattered.

Rose was sitting in her easy chair, relaxing with a glass of Christian Brothers and Coke.

Rose needed some time to think, to clear her head. Boaz seemed to be moving too fast. It had been a few days since their sexual tryst, and Rose was feeling so much guilt and shame, and she couldn't understand why. She was single, he was single—so what was the problem? Something was missing.

Rose sat there, nursing her drink, thinking, thinking, thinking.

Her feelings hadn't changed until they'd slept together. It's as if she was someone else.

She liked Boaz, and from what she remembered, he was pretty good in bed. So why did everything feel all twisted?

Just as that thought was marinating in her mind, there was a knock at the door. Rose stood up and swayed just a tad. Her drink was setting in, and she felt a little tipsy. After opening the door without asking who it was, Rose's joy turned into pure unbridled passion when she saw the fine specimen of man standing on the other side of the threshold.

"Hey, Rosie, baby, I was on this side, and I missed you. I just had to see you," Boaz crooned.

Rose grinned, pulled Boaz through the door, wrapped her arms around his thick neck, and placed a long passionate kiss on his lips. Boaz returned the kiss just as passionately.

The scent of Polo that engulfed Rose was intoxicating. Or was it the Christian Brothers? Maybe it was a combination of the two. Boaz closed the door behind him with his free hand as he was still in Rose's passionate embrace. Rose led Boaz to the bedroom, undressing him along the way. Rose was bewitched, and she didn't try to fight it. After consummating their visit, Rose lay in Boaz's arms, feeling like she had just won the lottery.

"Rosie, baby, I was gon' take you out to the movies tonight, but my check didn't get deposited on time."

Before Boaz could get another lie out, Rose said, "Oh it's okay, baby. This one will be on me."

Boaz burrowed himself deeper in the fluffy pillows and looked down with a wicked grin and said, "You sure, baby?" Before Rose had time to answer, he said, "Maybe we can hit Red Lobster afterward and before we go, I need to run by and pick up some clothes from the cleaners. I'll pay you back next week."

Rose just lay there, grinning.

Boaz hopped up. "You wanna anothter drink, Rosie?"

"No, baby."

"Well, how about fixin' me one?" Boaz sternly asked, heading for the shower.

Rose sat up, shook her head, and thought about what she'd just heard. Then she thought about what she'd just felt and proceeded to fix her man a drink.

"No-good, no-count, lyin' litte bitch! Tony, I don't know what in the hell you meant! I don't know what in the hell I meant! I should a never let you bring that ho in my house wit them two little bastards!" Miss Mamie barked as Tony sat at the kitchen table with his head hung in shame.

Rose May had been gone a week, eight days to be exact. Tony hadn't heard a thing. He didn't even know where to look. He didn't have time to look. Tony had to take some vacation days in order to take care of the boys. He knew his mother wasn't going to help. She hated Rose May and her seeds.

Tony paced the floor as he listened to his mother's vicious attacks on Rose May. Tony didn't have a clue as to what he should do. He had taken his last vacation day on Friday, and he knew by Sunday something had to be done.

If he wasn't at work on Monday, he knew he would be fired. Tony had been at UPS for ten years, and he certainly didn't want to loose his good-payin' job, as his mother called it.

Tony didn't know why he put up with Rose May. She treated him like a dog. He loved her. He genuinely loved Rose May. He'd loved her since she was a chunky little girl at Aunt Minnie's liquor house. He felt like he had an obligation to take care of Rose May and the boys, and he knew he would, especially now since he was becoming a real daddy, not just a baby daddy.

Rose May would become his wife. He would adopt Elijah, Ezra, and they would live happily ever after. There was just one major thing—well, two major things standing in the way of his perfect family: dope and his momma! Tony couldn't keep Rose May off drugs long enough for her to grasp the concept of being his wife, and even if he could, he would have to kill his momma before marrying Rose May.

"Tony! Tony! Tony! What you gonna do? You can't stay out of work and keep these chaps! You'll lose yo good-payin' job!" Mamie proclaimed. "I told you that ho wasn't no damn goo. Who leave they children like that . And that po' one in her belly! Po' lil' baby don't know nothing. That ho ain't havin' no gran' chap of mine! That ain't yo baby boy. She done laid that baby to ya!" Miss Mamie huffed as Tony sat there at the kitchen table, looking puzzled.

Tony knew something had to be done. But what? The only thing that made any sense was to call Granma Rose. Tony hated to do that. He hadn't really talked to her since Rose May and the boys moved in. Rose had such faith and confidence in him. What would he say? She expected him to take care of Rose May and the boys. Tony looked over at the phone on the wall, then looked over at his mother, whose lips were moving. But he didn't hear a thing. He was too embedded in his thought of calling Rose.

"Tony! Tony! Antonio May the Third! I know you hear me talking! You better get yo shit together, boy!" Mamie spewed in a very determined tone.

"Nih, you get yo ass up and find these children somewhere to go! I know I should have never let that girl in here… go on now! I ain't putting them up another night!"

Tony moved like a mechanical man toward the slim line phone perched on the kitchen wall. He hated to make the phone call, but Rose May had left no choice. As he reached for the phone, Tony was hoping that by some chance the phone would ring, and it would be Rose May, and he would go get her, and they wouldn't have to even worry Grandma Rose. She would never even have to know about this.

"Why you movin' so slow! Give me that damn phone!" Mamie spat, grabbing the phone from the wall before Tony could.

"What's the number? I'm calling her damn momma! Something gotta be did right now! Now give me that number!" Mamie said, pursing her lips together tightly.

"I'll call Grandma Rose, Momma," Tony replied hesitantly.

"Grandma? You damn right grandma! I ain't they damn grandma! That's who they supposed to be wit! You ain't they damn daddy!" Mamie cried.

Tony reached for the phone and looked at his mother who was breathing like a bull ready to charge. He knew he definitely didn't have a choice when he saw the rage in his mother's eyes. Tony's sweaty fingers dialed Rose's telephone number under duress.

Ring, ring, ring, ring—after the fourth ring, Tony hung up.

"Why you hang up?" Mamie roared.

"Nobody there," Tony said nonchalantly.

"Well, you better pack dem chaps up an' drop um off! It's over! They ain't staying here another damn night!" Mamie announced as she stormed out of the kitchen.

Tony turned to go up stairs and commence packing. He was sad. All his hopes and dreams were torn away from him in eight short days. He had a pang that pierced his heart as he gazed over at Ezra and Elijah who were sleeping. *Why?* Tony thought to himself. *Why? Why wasn't he enough for Rose May?*

As Tony proceeded to pack Rose May's things, thoughts on how to repair this shambled relationship raced through his mind. Nothing. Nothing.

After packing up the last of the boys' clothes, he knew he had no choice but to drive over to Grandma Rose's. Tony sat on the edge of the bed and placed his head in his hands and sobbed quietly. He really felt like letting out a loud wail, but he knew his momma would curse him out. Tony was hurt, hurt all over again.

Rose felt like she was in a dream. *Is this really me? Am I really lying here in this man's bed?* Rose rambled on in her head.

Rose cracked open one of her puffy bloodshot eyes and peeped over at Boaz, who was sleeping soundly. As Rose cracked open the other eye, which was just as red puffy as the other, her head clanged on the inside like a bunch of pots and pans banging together. Rose glanced over at the nightstand, which painted a vague picture of what took place the night before. Rose squeezed her eyes together tightly trying to replay the events of the night before. As hard as she tried, Rose was still hazy about last night.

The tape that Rose was playing in her head stopped when Boaz rolled over and pulled her snuggly up against him. Rose loved the way he felt next to her. His skin so soft, smelling so good.

Rose felt Boaz's breath slide across the back of her neck.

"Mornin', sugah," Boaz's husky voice moaned in Rose's ear.

"How about a little Sunday morning breakfast in bed?" Boaz crooned, sliding on top of Rose.

Rose almost got lost until she heard the word *Sunday*. The word Sunday brought an end to Boaz's anticipated tryst.

Rose jumped out of bed abruptly. "Boaz, it's Sunday mornin'. You know I gotta usher. I didn't even iron my dress!" Rose fussed on, "I told you I was goin' home last night! I told you I didn't want no damn Blue Helicopter!" Rose was getting wound up scrambling around the room, picking up pieces of clothing she didn't remember coming out of.

"It's Blue Motorcycle, baby." Boaz laughed. "Come on, back to bed, baby. We got plenty of time to be holy," Boaz crooned as he lept off the bed and pulled Rose sternly toward him.

Rose was clearly perturbed when Boaz threw her down on the bed. "Boaz, I gotta go home and get ready for church now!" Rose said.

"You gotta get ready for me!" Boaz bellowed.

Rose looked up into Boaz's eyes as his big frame straddled her, and for an instant, she could have sworn she didn't know who he was. His eyes were someone else's. When Boaz retrieved the frightened look in Rose's eyes, he eased up and pretended to be playing.

Rose slid from underneath him, looking sideways, continuing to collect her clothes as she scooted in the bathroom and quickly closed the door.

"Uuhh, Rose, baby. Uuuh, you know I was just playing, don't you?" Boaz stammered. Boaz listened intensely with his ear pressed tightly against the door. All he heard was running water. *Knock, knock, knock.* "You okay? Rosie, Rosie. Rosie, come on now, baby," Boaz pleaded.

Rose snatched open the door fully dressed. Rose looked up at Boaz angrily and said, "Nigga, don't you ever in yo life handle me like that no more. My daddy didn't put his hands on me like that, and you ain't either!" Rose raced past Boaz, grabbed her Gucci bag, and slammed the door on her way out.

Boaz glanced over at his well-toned naked body's reflection in the dresser mirror, grinned wickedly, and began to stroke himself seductively. "I like a little spice and emnity. It makes for real good and kinky make up sex."

After Boaz had finished pleasuring himself, he lay back, lit a cigarette, and thought about what color he'd wear to church this morning. He was on the finance committee and had to make a speech during the collection (offering). "White," Boaz said aloud to himself. He remembered Rose had to usher this morning, and she would be in white. Boaz knew she would get over this morning's little spat, and he knew just how she would get over it. He'd decided he would begin his seduction this very morning right in the Mount Jubillee Missionary Baptist Church's pulpit.

Boaz flicked on his cassette deck and began to groove to the smooth sounds of Marvin Gaye singing "Got to Give

It Up." Boaz popped his fingers and began to pick out his all-white ensemble. He knew it would knock Rose off her feet, especially the fact that he was dressed in all-white just as she was. Boaz eyed the all-white ensemble that he'd laid out across the bed. He knew that by the end of the day, his white suit would be laid across Rose's easy chair, his white shoes would be under her bed, and Rose would be under him.

Rose stepped out of the shower and began to dry off. Rose's legs and back were aching. She felt as though she'd been beaten up and slung around.

Rose went in the kitchen and put on a fresh pot of coffee. She looked up at the clock. *Seven o'clock*, Rose thought. She still had plenty of time before she had to be at her usher's post. Rose sat down at her kitchen table, let out a deep sigh, and stared at the coffee that had begun dripping in the pot.

Rose May, her mind moaned. Then it quickly snapped to Boaz. Rose's brow furrowed as she thought about the incident that had occurred "way over in the shank of the morning," as her grandmother would say.

"That nigga must be crazy," Rose said aloud as she got up to retrieve a coffee cup from the cabinet. Rose poured the hot black coffee in her cup, replaced the pot on the warmer, took her cup over to the table, and cradled the cup in her hands. Rose raised the coffee to her nose and breathed in a big whiff of the Folgers Dark Roast. It was her favorite brand. As God's sunlight spilled into the window on Rose, she felt the warmth on her face. She felt like she was having coffee with a friend. Rose's spirit began to ask her questions, *Do you really think that was acceptable? Do you really think you should be laying up? Don't you think you're drinking a little too much? Do you really think Boaz is the man for you? Where is Rose May? Don't you think you should call her?*

The questions flooded her like a river. Rose shook her head quickly, as if trying to shake her conscience free. Rose hadn't talked to the Good Master in a while. Rose let out a deep sigh, looked up at the ceiling, and began to pray, "Lord, you know me. This Rose. I'm sorry, Lord. I'm sorry I ain't talked to ya in a while. Truth is, Lord, I been ashamed. I'm ashamed of myself. Lord, please forgive me. I'm goin' to yo house today, Lord, and I'm gon' get back right, Lord. I am and I'm gon' call Rose May, my seed. And, Lord, I'm gon' quit Boaz. Amen."

Just as Rose reached for the phone to call Rose May, the door bell rang. Rose jumped up, looked through the peep hole, sighed, and smiled. It was Bessie. Rose let her in.

Bessie burst through the door excitedly.

"Girrrl, you ain't dressed yet? You know we gotta usher. You been wit that fine Boaz last night, ain't you?"

Before Rose had time to answer, Bessie pulled her to the table, sat down, crossed her legs, and put on her listening ears.

"Tell me, girl, tell me." Bessie urged.

"Come on, now, Bessie. I ain't got time for all that. I ain't even ironed my dress," Rose said, walking toward the closet with Bessie right on her heels.

"Go on and get ready. I'll iron, you talk. Tell me now," Bessie coaxed as she pulled the ironing board from the closet, set it up, and laid the white usher's uniform face down on it.

"It really ain't much to tell, Bessie," Rose said very shamefully as she sat down at her vanity to put on her white stockings.

Bessie gave her a condescending look as she plugged in the iron. "Now, you know I know you, Rose Carlisle. I know that look. Now tell me what happened."

Rose stood up as she struggled to manipulate her panty hose up her sore thighs. Rose looked up, and her eyes locked with Bessie's.

"What?" Rose quipped. Bessie continued to iron, staring at Rose.

"Okay, okay, okay," Rose said, clearly defeated by her best friend's discernment. "Me and Boaz had a fight," Rose spilled.

"A fight? What you mean, a fight?" Bessie said, almost dropping the iron.

Rose led Bessie through the scenario.

"Aw, child, is that all? That ain't nothing," Bessie said matter-of-factly as she continued to iron. "All couples fuss a little."

"It was more than that," Rose said as she applied her clear lip gloss and fluffed her hair. "It was like he was somebody else, Bessie. That nigga would have scared me if I was the scary type," Rose said as she reached for the heavily starched dress Bessie had ironed.

"Well, y'all will kiss and make up and everything will be fine," Bessie said.

"I don't know about this time, Bessie," Rose said as she put on her dress and snapped on her usher's pin. "Something just don't feel right."

"Well, all I know is you don't need to be worrying about nothing as small as that. Good of a man as you got," Bessie quipped. "Come on, girl, I don't wanna be late. I wanna stop by Hardee's and get me a steak biscuit."

Rose slipped on her white pumps, grabbed her white purse, and trailed after Bessie but not before looking up at the ceiling reminding her of the promises she'd made to God.

The crowd at Mount Jubilee Missionary Baptist was jumping this first Sunday morning. Rose and Bessie were extra busy as they passed out fans and worked with the spirit-filled congregants that had gotten happy and shouted as the choir sang their hyped-up version of "Do Not Pass Me By."

Rose hadn't had time to look over in the deacon's corner to see Boaz's lustful looks following her from pew to pew. Rose really meant business. She was mad at Boaz, and it was over. She meant what she said, and she said what she meant. That was until they called for the offering and Deacon Boaz Brown stepped up in the pulpit, wearing his all-white Armani suit with the white alligator Stacy Adams to match.

Rose stood at her usher's post and looked up in the pulpit as the good Deacon Brown delivered his finance report. Rose tried as hard as she could to stay in church-usher mode, but all she could see was that fine black man naked in the pulpit. Rose looked down at her feet and shuffled her fans awkwardly as their eyes met. Rose knew he was undressing her as he stood up and eloquently gave his speech. Rose grew hot, and she knew her face began to blush. She took out one of her fans and fanned fiercely.

Rose was ashamed, but ashamed of who? Nobody in the church knew she and Boaz had been dating. She didn't feel they should announce it yet. "Hmph!" Rose grunted as she continued to fan and watch the white suited-demon beguile his audience. Boaz finished his speech and called the ushers forth to take the collection. Rose headed down the aisle and felt Deacon Brown's eyes like heat all over her. Boy was she ashamed as she approached the altar.

As Rose reached up for the offering plate, Deacon Brown gave Rose's hand a slight rub as he passed the plate.

Rose gulped loudly as she swallowed and turned to take up the collection. She was hot. Why was it so hot in here? Rose felt beads of sweat roll down the back of her neck as she went from pew to pew, retrieving the collection plate. When Rose reached the last pew, collected her plate, turned around, and walked down the aisle toward the offering table, Boaz didn't take his eyes off her. Rose felt naked as she walked before the congregation to bless the offering. She was so ashamed as she and Boaz stood there side by side. She couldn't help but catch a whiff of the pungent Hugo Boss that filled the air next to her. Honestly, it made her tingle. She was so ashamed to be lusting in the house of the Lord.

Rose took her seat after the choir sang two selections, and she and the other ushers had calmed everybody down. Rose sat and listened intensely as Reverend Baker preached from Proverbs 26 about sin being exposed. Rose curled up her toes in her pointed toe pump because Reverend Baker was definitely stepping on her toes. Boaz amened and amened again as Reverend Baker brought his sermon home with a few ahas. As the sermon closed, Reverend Baker opened the altar up for the altar call. He called for all who wanted to be saved, know Jesus, and have their name written in the Lamb's Book of Life. He also called for backsliders.

Rose couldn't move. She was stuck. As the choir sang "Remember Me Oh Lord," Rose just kept her eyes closed. She could feel Boaz, looking. Rose slipped off the back pew and out the double door. She didn't worry about Bessie getting home. She could find a ride. Rose didn't feel like mingling after church anyway. Rose was ashamed, very ashamed as she walked quickly to her car. Just as she was about to slip the key in the door, she caught a whiff of Hugo Boss engulf her nostrils.

"Wait a minute, Sister Carlisle," the church voice called.

Rose spun around to see Deacon Brown dead in her face. *He is sooo fine*, Rose thought, still keeping her stern face.

"Yes, Deacon Brown. What is it?" Rose said sternly.

"Can I come by and see you later?" Boaz whispered through clenched teeth.

Rose just looked and shook her head yes. Boaz turned and walked away with a look of triumph on his face. Rose got in the car, slammed the door, and sat there for a moment, not even realizing what she had just done. It happened so fast. She really meant to say no. She really meant to go up to that altar and rededicate her life. She was mesmerized. When Boaz came around, it's like she was in a trance. Rose started her car, put it in drive, and commenced driving home to get ready for her after-church, Sunday night rendezvous.

Tony piled the last of Rose May's and the boy's things into his chevy. Tony had always loved Sundays because he just felt renewed. Even though Tony hadn't been brought up in the church, he knew there had to be a God. Tony had visited Mount Jubilee Missionary Baptist with Rose May and her mother. He loved it the few he did attend.

One Sunday, he almost got his name written in the Lamb's Book of Life. Tony would often sit and ponder that Sunday and ask himself why he didn't take that trip down the aisle when Reverend Baker opened up altar call. Tony believed there was a God. He even thought about Jesus and the stories he was told about Him in Sunday school. Tony just never took the time to learn about Him. He especially loved Sundays because of Grandma Rose's great Sunday feasts.

Tony looked up at the clouds and whimsically smiled as he thought of how he, Rose May, and Grandma Rose would sit down at the dinner table that was filled with every Sunday delicacy imagined and laugh and talk for hours. Tony's smile evaporated and turned serious as he thought about this God he had fleetingly heard of here and there.

Tony began, "God or Jesus or I 'ont even know…Could you please look after Rose May wherever she is…Look after my boys and especially the one that ain't here yet. Uuuuh, thank you, sir."

Tony slammed the chevy door and proceeded up the walk to get Ezra and Elijah who were patiently waiting by the steps. Tony had decided he would take the boys out to dinner. This would give Rose May a little more time before he dropped them off. After Tony had everybody buckled in, he drove off, still hoping that maybe there was still a chance for his happily ever after.

Rose May's mind was still closed. She had been shacked up with her present baby daddy/momma for about two weeks now. Or was it three? Rose May had lost track of the days, the hours, the minutes, and the seconds. Rose May and Danni had smoked so much crack, smoked so much weed, drank so much Canadian Mist, Seagram's Gin, White Lightnin', Wild Irish Rose, snorted so much powder, and screwed so many men and women, they were delirious.

Rose May peeped through Danni's bedroom door very cautiously and whispered, "Danni, Danni." Rose May finally yelled, "Danyale! You sleep?"

"Heell, naw, bitch!" Danni proclaimed, popping up from under the tangled covers that lay atop his massive king-sized bed. "I aint sleep. I'm geeked!" Danni stated as he reached over on the nightstand, held up his glass stem toward the light, rolled it between his red hot, red-painted fingertips to survey its contents.

"We ain't got no more dope. We gotta get fresh and get on it," Rose May announced, rubbing her oversized belly.

"We sure the hell do! You know Momma gotta have her base," Danni said as he fumbled in the nightstand drawer for a pusher to clean out his overworked shooter.

"Why you messing wit' dat bullshit? We need a fresh pack, and I know just where to get some fire," Rose May said.

"Where?" Danni asked, stretching the burnt crumbly black chore boy he had fished out of his shooter.

"Just come on! We ain't got time to be bullshittin' around, Danni!" Rose May said as she grimaced and grabbed her stomach.

"Whats wrong? I know you ain't finna' have that damn baby. You got two more months, don't you?" Danni asked, still engrossed in his task.

"Hell, naw, it's just gas, and I need my medicine. I'm sick! Now let's get our shit together so we can get on!" Rose May pleaded, heading for the bathroom.

"Okay, okay. Let me just push my jimmie an' I'll be ready," he pleaded. Danni sat on the bed, pushing and packing, packing and pushing, trying to salvage just one more hit from the cracked burned shooter.

"Ooooh, shit! Damn! Oh no." Rose May's voice resonated from the bathroom.

"What is it, honey!" Danni asked, dropping the overworked stem from his mouth as he rushed over to press his ear against the door. "What's wrong boo?"

"I need to go to the hospital! Something's coming out!" Rose May shrieked.

"Hold on! Hold on. Hold on, nih!" Danni screamed, turning around in circles.

"Just go get the car, Danni," Rose May yelled.

Danni slipped on his leopard jumpsuit; slid on his platform clogs; retrieved his number 1B/27 wig from the dresser; and headed out the door, Louis Vitton bag in hand; and sprinted for the car.

Rose May sat on the toilet, grimacing from the pain and pressure that was coming from her belly. She looked up and began to talk to God through clenched teeth, "God, please don't let this happen right now! It ain't time. I don't want this damn baby, especially not right now."

Danni returned, feverishly knocking on the door. "Come on, bitch! I got the car around front."

Rose May managed to pull herself up off the toilet, open the door, and fall into Danni's waiting arms.

Danni struggled to keep Rose May steady as he held her up in a rather manly fashion. After Rose May was laid in the backseat of car, Danni hopped in the driver's seat and proceeded to the hospital, but not before lighting up a freshly rolled blunt.

"Girl, you wanna hit this?" Danni asked, holding up the blunt.

"Hell, yeah," Rose May painfully answered, holding out her shaky hand.

Danni passed the blunt over the seat. As Danni dug off to the hospital, Rose May lay in the back seat, pulling the blunt with full force, absorbing every drop off smoke, holding it in until she couldn't any longer. As Rose May released the smoke, she thought of what was to come. It was too complicated to play the whole tape, so she shook her head, lay back, ferociously sucked the blunt, and waited for the next move.

Rose made a beeline for the kitchen cabinet as soon as she shot through the front door. She dropped her purse and keys on the couch, kicking her shoes off as she approached the corner cabinet. Rose stood on tiptoe, reached for the special bottle, unscrewed the top, put the bottle to her lips, threw her head back, and felt the warm brown liquid cover her throat. It burned in a good way as it travelled down her throat and hit the bottom of her stomach. Rose slammed the bottle on the cabinet and smacked her lips.

Why did I let that nigga come over? Now I gotta fix something for dinner, Rose fussed to herself as she looked in the freezer. She took out a roast and threw it in the sink. Just as she turned to retrieve another gulp from her full bottle of Christian Brothers, the doorbell rang. Rose smacked her teeth and headed to answer the door. Rose peeped through the peephole to see Bessie standing on the other side with pot in her hand.

"Hey, girl," Bessie greeted as she walked through the door after Rose opened it.

"Hey, Bessie," Rose dryly replied.

"What's wrong wit you? I smell you done hit the special bottle already," Bessie stated, placing her pot of collard greens on the stove. "Where yo glass at? Take another wit me!" Bessie requested.

"I don't need a glass," Rose said, holding up the bottle for display.

"Oooo, child. This is serious," Bessie sad, grabbing the bottle in midair and pouring herself a drink.

The two women sat down at the kitchen table, still in their usher uniforms, and began to talk. "Girrrrrrrl, I saw that fine deacon of yours, looking at you awwwl through the service," Bessie yelped after throwing back a shot of Christian Brothers.

"I know, child," Rose said, feeling a warm sensation fall over her face. "He was awwwl over me!" Rose giggled.

Rose rared back in her chair, crossed her white stockinged-legs, and her spirit filled up with a schoolgirl charm. She began to grin and think about the fine lover she had, coming over in just a few hours.

"What you all grinning-faced for?" Bessie asked, pouring herself a double. "Oh, Oh, I know, reverend deacon coming over, 'aint he? I thought you was soo mad?" Bessie said with a slight slurr in her voice.

"I am," Rose gulped. "That's th best time for making up!" Rose let out a yelping laugh, slapping her thigh. The two women hollered and gave each other a high five.

"Well, I guess I better get on thru so you can get yourself together for yo man," Bessie jeered.

"You ain't gotta go yet, Bessie. You just got here. Stay and have a plate and maybe another drink or two," Rose insisted.

"Well, you ain't gotta ask me twice." Bessie quickly obliged, getting up to stir the pot of collards she donated to the dinner.

Rose was feeling kind of good by the time she decided to get up and flip on the cassette deck.

As Bessie heard the lead singer of The Manhattans croon the first verse of "It feels so good to be loved so bad," she let out an "Oooh, child. That's my song!" as the smooth melody reached her ears. She and Rose met in the living room, giving each other a tipsy high five.

"You know you sure are lucky, Rose, to have somebody to cuddle up wit every now and then," Bessie said, looking down in her shot glasses very forlornly, rubbing her finger around the rim of it.

"Bessie, you'll find somebody. Just wait on the Good Master like I did," Rose said, leaning over to gently stroke her misty-eyed friend's hand.

Bessie snapped out of her trance, jumped up, snapped her fingers, and began to slow drag by herself.

"You so crazy, girl!" Rose exclaimed as she jumped up and headed toward the bedroom.

Rose sat at her vanity and stared at her reflection. Why was she keeping up this masquerade? She knew good and well what she'd promised the Lord. She knew she didn't need to be drinking, especially on a Sunday. She also knew she had a sinking feeling in her gut, and it wasn't the brandy. Rose began to feel the brandy warm her body as she peeled off her brandy-stained usher's dress. Rose looked over at her bed and pictured Boaz lying on her big fluffy pillows. Rose was really trying, but she just couldn't shake the sinking feeling she was having. It was like something was about to happen. Rose just shook it off and zeroed her attention in on the front room where Bessie had changed tapes and was listening to the upbeat sounds of Con Funk Shun's "Shake and Dance With Me." She heard Bessie pick up the phone and dial a number.

"Can you talk?" Bessie whispered. "How long? You ain't lying this time, are you?" Bessie begged on. "Okay, see ya soon." *Click.*

Rose listened on and heard the tape change to Marvin Sease and Millie Jackson singing "Slow Rolling." Rose knew then that the call Bessie had made was to the very prestigious Deacon Haywood and the very married Deacon Haywood. Rose never understood, and no matter how many times she and Bessie had discussed it, Bessie loved a married man. Rose looked over at the clock, four o'clock. The phone rang.

"Rose?" Bessie happily yelled down the hall. "It's yo man," she giggled.

Rose reached over and picked up the receiver. "Hello."

"Hey, Rosie, baby," Boaz's husky, sexy voice greeted.

"Hi," Rose said, looking up at the ceiling.

"You ready for me, baby? You sure looked sweet today in all that white. I can't wait to see you."

"Really?" Rose solemnly stated.

"Why you sounding like that? You been sippin'. Wait on me. You know I'm BYOB. Hello? Hello?" Boaze echoed. "Why you ain't sayin' nothing, baby? I know you ain't still mad about last night. Come on, sweetie. Big daddy will be there, and I'll make everything all right," the husky voice growled.

Rose felt a tingle go through her as she listened. Something inside her turned to putty, and she whispered, "Okay, I'll see you."

As Rose reached over to return the receiver, she heard Boaz's voice elevating each time, saying, "Hey, hey, Rosie, baby."

Rose put the phone to her ear and said, "Yes baby?"

"Have my plate ready when I get there." *Click.*

Rose just sat there staring at the phone in her hand.

Rose knew deep in her heart of hearts that she should not let Boaz come over. But there was an overwhelming desire in her to have him. Rose ignored her heart of hearts and skipped off to run her bathwater.

Rose May was high as cooter brown when Danni turned in to Mercy Hospital's emergency room entrance on two wheels.

"We here, bitch!" Danni yelled as he scrambled from the car and reeled over on one of his clogs. "Help! Help! Help!" he yelled, looking toward the sliding glass, double doors as he pulled Rose May from the rear seat. Two nurses rushed out with a wheelchair and carefully placed Rose May in it.

"Don't y'all hurt my boo now! Be careful, be careful." Danni snapped as he filtered around the two nurses, snapping his fingers.

One of the two nurses looked down at Rose May and asked, "What's wrong with her?" The other nurse looked over and said, "She's stoned for one thing!"

Danni rolled his neck and said, "Ain't a damn thing wrong wit her but gotta have a damn baby! Now you handle wit care." Danni snapped and motioned for the nurse to keep it moving.

Rose May rolled her head back, looked up at Danni, and slurred, "Don't leave me, boo. Don't leave me."

"Couldn't nothing but death keep me from it!" Danni emphatically stated, snapped two times in the air, doing his model walk as the nurses followed with Rose May in tow.

Rose May was taken straight to the fourth floor and admitted. In Rose May's room, Danni stood by her bedside, holding her friend's hand.

"Girrrrl, you gon' be just fine. This type of thing happen every day."

"Not to me." Rose May looked up and timidly said, "You think I should call my momma. I'm scared, Danni. I don't think I'm gon' make it thru this one."

"Well, I tell you one thing. You call Momma Rose up here while I'm in here, and I'll be rolled down to that emergency room I'm sure with a concussion." Danni said, pursing his lips, "I'm here for you girl. You know you my partner. We gon' always be down, boo! I love you. We been down a long time, shuga!" Danni proclaimed, leaning down to give Rose May a quick peck on the forehead.

"Well, in that case," Rose May said between contractions. "There's something I need to tell you."

"What, boo? You know I love to death," Danni said, fluttering his long eyelashes.

"You remember the time…," just as Rose May started to tell Danni the baby's doctor came through the door. Rose May was in labor, and she should be prepped for delivery.

Danni blinked his eyes and fanned himself emphatically with his jeweled hand as the doctor left the room.

"Girrrl, we gone have us a baby, boo!" he dramatically whimpered.

Rose May looked up at her transvestite friend who was holding her hand so tenderly. She quickly tugged ideas around in her head on how she should break the news to Danni that they were both about to become new mommies. Rose May was high, seriously. Several thoughts flooded her mind in what seemed like seconds. She thought about her momma, wondering if she was still lost in that man. She thought about Tony and his mean-ass, nasty momma. She thought about the good Reverend Jeremiah Jones, black bastard. She thought about Reno, psycho bitch. She thought about Elijah, Ezra, her little seeds. Just as quickly as the thoughts entered, with the last one that entered Rose May burst out…

"That night when you was ballin', and we did a show for that square white dude," Rose May stopped, took a big deep breath in, and exhaled with her words. "The condom broke. I got pregnant, and you the daddy."

Danni's hand stopped fanning in midair, his eyes widened, his mouth fell upon, and *bam!* He hit the floor.

Rose May leaned over the bed rail, looked down at the floor, and saw Danni spread-eagled, clogs off, and his 1B27 wig twisted to the side of his head like a baseball cap.

She fell back on the pillow, looked upward, and began to ball like a big baby. Rose May was in the biggest pickle ever, and as a famous song once said, "All she could do was cry."

Rose emerged from the bathtub, dripping with the scent of Chanel N°5. Rose loved Chanel N°5. It was her favorite fragrance. She sat down at her vanity and remembered she'd left Bessie up front, grooving hard.

"Bessie? You okay, girl?" Rose yelled out while applying her body oil.

"Yeah, girl, I almost got this dinner together. I'm gon' take a plate wit me. I gotta go see a man about a horse." Bessie snickered.

Rose looked up smiled and said, "Yeah right."

Rose felt like a mechanical woman as she went through the motions of getting ready for her hot date. She sat on the edge of her bed, opened the nightstand drawer to make sure all of the bedroom essentials, as Boaz called them, were there.

Rose really didn't like all the extra stuff Boaz liked. She liked just plain old making love. Maybe in few different position every now and then, but not to the extent that she was receiving minor injures. The past few times Rose had been with Boaz, she'd woke up the next morning, feeling like she had been under vicious attack—bruises, aches, and pains. The last time, she'd remembered lovemaking didn't feel like that! Rose slammed the drawer, almost getting mad. She looked down at her ankle, which was slightly bruised. She thought about another aspect of her and Boaz's lovemaking, his dirty talk. In the beginning, a few little minor dirty words turned her on.

Boaz had gotten a little too dirty the last few times. She also hated when he would ask "You gone gimme some coochie?"

What is coochie? And who asks a grown woman that? Rose thought, twisting her eyebrows downward.

It wasn't just the physical things. Rose was beginning to feel drained. She felt bounded up on the inside. Her mind began to race as she looked over at the heart-shaped photographs of Ezra and Elijah. She missed them. She missed Rose May. She knew Rose May was in a pickle. She could feel it. Rose stood up with a determination in her spirit. She would tell Boaz this Sunday night how she felt. She felt like they needed a little space. She needed some time. Some time to figure out what was going on.

Rose grabbed up the slinky white negligee she had laid out on the bed, balled it up, and crammed it in her drawer. "I won't be needing this," Rose said as she slammed the drawer shut.

"And why not?" a sexy voice bellowed from behind.

Rose jumped as she turned to see Boaz standing in the doorway.

"I did ninety all the way here just to get to yo fine ass," the deacon's sexy voice spewed. Boaz walked over, grabbed Rose up in his big strong arms, pulled her close, and rubbed his tongue up the side of her neck.

Rose's knees got weak, and she was like a limp rag doll in his arms, panting breathlessly.

"Where's Bessie?" Rose whispered.

"Gone," Boaz said, walking Rose over to the bed without loosing his grip.

Rose was hot, real hot. She felt like she was being devoured as Boaz kissed her up and down her neck.

"Boaz," Rose said breathlessly, "We need to talk."

"Baby, we will, we will. Just let me love you!" Boaz insisted, undressing Rose as he spoke.

"Okay," Rose mindlessly replied, switching off the lamp and letting Boaz do just as he's requested.

After Rose and Boaz had both been fully satisfied, Rose lie in her man's arms, not thinking of any of her previous grievances. All she was thinking about was the fine man who, unbeknownst to her, was a sick, creepy pervert. Not only that. He's just deposited another load of demons into her spirit.

Just as Rose got up to freshen up, the doorbell rang.

"Who the hell is that?" Boaz replied, rolling over to open the nightstand drawer.

Rose glanced at him, realizing he was getting revved up for round two, kinky mode.

Rose hurriedly slid on her slippers, grabbed her rope, put it on, and headed for the front door. But not before Boaz grabbed the hem of her rope, begging her to ignore it.

Rose popped her lips, rolled her eyes, and proceeded to answer the bell, which had turned into incessant knocking.

"Tony!" Rose said after snatching the door open. "What's wrong? Where's Rose May? Where the babies?" Rose asked worriedly. "Come on in, Tony, where they at?" she asked again.

"The boys in the car. Let me go get them," Tony replied very solemnly.

Rose watched and waited anxiously as Tony turned to retrieve the babies.

"Who is it?" Boaz's voice shouted up the hall.

"Hold on, Boaz. It's Tony," Rose said, waving her arm, snubbing him off.

"Who?" he asked again.

"Tony! I'll be there in a minute!" she said, slightly perturbed.

Tony returned with two sleeping bundles in his arms.

"Ooooh, my babies," Rose squealed as she reached for the bundles.

"Ganma missed them babies, yes she did," Rose said, talking baby talk. Rose put the two sleeping babies on the couch and returned her attention to Tony, who looked like he was going through the Valley of Baka.

As Rose walked over to close the front door, her stomach began to quake. She peeped out the door looking upward toward the heavens. Rose began a quick prayer of distress in her head, "Oh, Father, Father, Father, Good Master. Oh, Lily of the Valley, I need you. I know I'm gon' hear something bad. Just help me, Lord."

Rose closed the door, snapped the lock, turned to look at Tony, and knew by the look on his face—coupled with the roar in stomach—she needed to prepare for war.

CPSIA information can be obtained at www.ICGtesting.com
Printed in the USA
LVOW10s1333010716

494831LV00003B/4/P